Endorsements for Dear Pakistan

a CBCA Notable Book

Terrific that you are writing a story around this theme [of third culture kids]. This updates the Dyers attempts back in the 1980s and 1990s. Look forward to reading Dear Pakistan. This will be an invaluable addition to the literature. Will circulate in the missions community in Australia and beyond.

David Turnbull, Senior Lecturer in Intercultural Studies

In an incredibly unique and yet genuine and readable way this book gives insight into cross-cultural work, some of the challenges encountered, and – I have discovered – can really help people as well as be an enjoyable read. I especially have recommended it to teens & young adults who have been involved or will be involved themselves cross-culturally, or who are children of cross-cultural workers. I say this not only from the experience of others but also my own.

Sean Boucher, WEC International

Rosanne Hawke often writes movingly of relocation. She is able to engage the feelings of the reader as the main character goes through the trauma of separation and removal.

Fran Knight, Magpies

The strong character of Jaime will strike a chord with many teenagers who may feel they don't belong.

Tina Cavanough, Magpies

A beautifully crafted story and a memorable read.

Pegi Williams

This is the first book I have seen written from the perspective of a thoughtful girl who after learning to fit into an alien society has to go through the same process in her own. It's fascinating.

H Nowicka, Reading Time

A clever twist on the now well-worn theme of immigrant experience.

John Murray, Magpies

Dear Pakistan

Published by Rhiza Press
PO BOX 1519
Capalaba QLD 4157
Australia

Cover Design by Rhiza Press and Production Works
Layout by Rhiza Press

First edition published by Albatross Books, 1995.
Second edition published by Lothian books, 2003.
Third edition published by Rhiza Press, 2016.

National Library of Australia Cataloguing-in-Publication entry

Creator:	Hawke, Rosanne, author.
Title:	Dear Pakistan / Rosanne Hawke.
ISBN:	9781925139549 (paperback)
Series:	Hawke, Rosanne. Beyond borders ; 1.
Target Audience:	For young adults.
Subjects:	Australians--Pakistan--Fiction.
	Women--Pakistan--Fiction.
	Pakistan--Social life and customs--Fiction.
	Australia--Social life and customs--Fiction.
Dewey Number:	A823.3

Dear Pakistan

Rosanne Hawke

For all third culture kids,
especially Lenore, Michael and Emma

1

I knew I was in Australia when I noticed all the legs—men's legs! I never thought there could be so many variations: short, long, muscled, knobbly-kneed. Then there were the hairy ones. I think the thick curly red hairs fascinated me the most, that is, until Mum caught me staring.

'Jaime!' She looked shocked for a second, then grinned. 'Quite a sight, isn't it? I'm sorry, I forgot to warn you about the shorts. Men here wear them all the time in summer.'

The shocks didn't stop there. Meeting everyone in the airport lounge was like an elephant stampede. People whom I'd never met before called me by my name and hugged me—even the guys! Mum kept trying to introduce people.

'This is Aunty Pat, don't you remember? And this is your cousin John. Hasn't he grown?' Cousin John even kissed me! I managed to wipe it off when he wasn't looking. I think it's disgusting to kiss someone when you don't even know if they want you to or not.

Maybe Mum could see me begin to wilt, for she managed to steer us all out to the cars that were there to collect us. One was Papa's. He's our grandfather and I remembered him as he visited us in Pakistan. Poor Dad was still in a daze and my younger brother and sister managed to get pushed along like seaweed before a tide.

I can't even remember who got into the car with us, just that they talked a lot. I couldn't help thinking how clean everything was and what an orderly way everyone drove, with no horns blaring. It was like stepping onto another planet in a science fiction novel. Then I stopped thinking things like that. It made me feel guilty, as though I was being disloyal to Pakistan.

In no time we were at Mama's and Papa's. All I felt like doing was falling asleep and I could tell the rest of us felt the same but there were so many people. Some I remembered vaguely from photos and from coming back for my Aunty's wedding a few years before. They all seemed so pleased to see us. I know this sounds awful, but I got so sick of hearing, 'And this is Jaime? My word, quite the young lady now. And what do you think of Australia?'

And before I could say anything, even if I could think of anything (which I couldn't), they'd asked the next question, 'Do you miss Pakistan?'

What did they expect! I'd only been here an hour. I caught Mum watching me anxiously, so I just nodded and smiled. (Though I felt as smiley as a leopard about to pounce.) It was better when we moved into our own house in Salisbury. We used to live here years ago before we went to Pakistan and before Elly was born. The fishponds that Mum said I used to play in as a toddler were still there. Lots of people visited when we first moved back. Mum and Dad sure had heaps of friends. They were all so kind, but I never knew what to say and they always asked the wrong questions. The easiest one was: 'Why have you come back to Adelaide?' I knew the answer to that at least: 'Because I needed to finish high school here to get into uni, and my grandparents were missing us.'

I guess I kept trying to find something familiar and couldn't. There were eucalyptus trees like we had at home in Pakistan, and everyone drove on the left side of the road, but there the similarities ended. The neighbours here kept to themselves; girls wore short skirts, not to mention the guys' shorts!

One afternoon, Dad took us kids to the beach. That's one thing he'd missed in Pakistan. There was a young couple rolling around and kissing in the sand. I could hardly rip my eyes away, even though I was shocked. Dad was pretty disgusted, and bundled us back to the car, saying he must have been away from Australia longer than he thought. He made it sound as if the kids were doing something new. In Pakistan, the women cover up and if anyone did anything like that in public they'd most probably get whipped.

We'd only been home a week before school started and I wasn't looking forward to it. In Pakistan I'd gone to a co-ed international boarding school. I'd had so much fun, most of which was had after school hours. There was no way I could see how a private day school could compare with it.

This is what I wrote in my journal that first week.

~~Dear Journal~~

~~Dear Diary~~

Dear Pakistan

I'm going to write to you like I wrote to my diary last year. Mum says it helps to write everything that you feel so I can't think of anyone better to write it to than you. For you see, you are everything I miss and that I've left behind: my school, my friends—I miss Ayesha and Liana and Jasper so much. I also miss you too, dear Pakistan: your people, your mountains (there's not one in sight here) and the excitement in the air that was just you. Don't worry, I'll be back as soon as I get enough money saved up.

Jameela

P.S. It's so weird here. The men wear shorts all the time, even down the street and to church! You'd puke for sure!

P.P.S. Mum's picked up a stray kitten already. She's called it Basil, yet again. It's got one of those fluffy tails like the last Basil she adopted in Abbottabad.

2

I knew things weren't going too well at school when the third teacher made a smart comment about my nose pin. I didn't remember any of our family friends at the airport making comments, but maybe they'd been warned.

'Is that to lead you around by?' some little snot said at recess time. I didn't answer and walked on towards the canteen with what I hoped was a confident 'I've been here before' look on my face.

I did answer the girl who sat by me in maths, though. Her name was Sara.

'Why do you have a nose pin?' she asked.

She sounded as if she'd like one too, so I told her. 'In Pakistan, almost all the girls have it done, usually when they're about thirteen, but always before they're married. That's so they can wear the gold kokar in their nose, a chain goes across their cheek and up into their hair.'

After the first sentence, I could tell Sara didn't want to hear any more. I don't know why I kept going. Guess I just wanted someone to understand.

'I had it done in the local gold shop in the bazaar where we lived. The jeweller made the hole with a piece of silver that he'd sharpened. He poured aftershave all over my nose first and then he stuck it in. I nearly fainted, especially when he couldn't get it straight through the first time.'

The look of incredulous horror on Sara's face stayed with me for quite a while afterwards. She didn't ask me another personal question for months.

Lunchtime got worse. After the first 'What school did you go to?' and my answer, 'I went to a boarding school in Pakistan …' that was it. They'd jump in with what they saw on paid TV the night before, which really left me in the woods, because we didn't have much TV in Pakistan, certainly not Australian shows. So how was I to know who the Neighbours were or that Big Brother wasn't a sci-fi thriller? It sounded like one.

I shouldn't have tried to enter into the conversation, until I knew more. I know it sounds over the top but I felt as if I did know more than them. Maybe not about TV shows, but about things that matter. Yet the more mistakes I made, and the more they made fun of me, the more I felt as though I was the one in the wrong.

When the conversation moved onto movies, it was no better. Girls didn't go to the movies in Pakistan, and although the boarding school had showed movies Friday nights, they were very 'family orientated' and rarely recent releases. I was totally left out of the conversation and no one made an effort to draw me in. One girl even glanced at me as if I were up myself and I hadn't even opened my mouth.

Mum was in the kitchen when I got home from school. She gave me a big hug.

'How was it?' she asked with that look on her face as if she knew already.

'It was the pits. They all think Pakistan is part of India. One kid actually called me the new girl from Africa. And …' Here I launched into a few of the things that really did confuse me. Let Mum work out which ones bothered me the most. 'You should have heard the way they talk about their boyfriends. They all seem to have one and all they can think about is if he's 'cool' or got muscles and plays some sort of sport. I asked one girl if her boyfriend was kind and understood what she thought about.' I stopped for a breath.

'What did she say?' Mum actually sounded interested.

'She couldn't answer. It was like she'd never thought about it before, like "Why get that serious?" They even sleep with them. And you know what else?'

Mum raised her eyebrows. I knew she was just expecting more along the lines of 'sleeping with'. That hadn't seemed to bother her as much as I thought it would, but I knew I'd get her on this one. 'There's a condom machine in the toilet.'

With satisfaction, I saw Mum's jaw sag slightly before she controlled herself. She's usually unshockable, but I like to see how far she'll tolerate things.

'This is Australia.' I did an exaggerated bow. 'The land of the free. You don't get thrown into jail for what you believe here but it seems you can do whatever else you like. No rules.'

'There must be some,' Mum murmured, placating me now. She didn't need to worry, I wasn't about to change my rule system overnight. 'You'll have to listen harder. Don't say anything about yourself until you're asked—just listen.'

I stared at her, standing there, tea towel in hand. It was almost as though she'd been at school with me. 'How'd you know they didn't want to hear where I'd been?'

She turned on the oven. 'I've been down to the shops today and run into some people we knew. It's the same in any age group. We've come into their scene, Jaime. They like to call the shots. We just have to wait until someone is interested. All our close family and friends are, of course. But don't expect too much from the kids at school for a while. They've never travelled. They just don't understand.'

I gave Mum a quick hug. Andrew came in then and by the look on his face, I knew he must have felt like me. He most probably wouldn't tell Mum, though. He was the quiet type who hated to make a fuss. He'd get a hug, maybe longer than usual if he needed it, and then say everything was fine. I retreated to my bedroom. I didn't want to help Mum draw anything out of Andrew. I had enough to think about myself.

My little sister, Elly, was already in there.

'Who said you could come in my room?' I started in on the big-sister act until she burst into tears.

'The … the kids don't like me at school,' she managed between sobs.

'I think that makes three of us,' I murmured.

'What?' Elly was blowing her nose on my Winnie the Pooh tissues.

'Never mind.' I moved the box further away. 'What did they say?'

Elly swallowed down a sob. 'They swore all the time.'

I didn't know what to say. I guess the kids I was talking with swore too, but I didn't take much notice. What they were talking about seemed so much worse. I stood staring at her with her eyes all puffy and her French braid messed up. She was such a sweet kid. She had one of those brains that computed everything into certain boxes so she saw everything in black and white, wrong and right.

'It was so awful, Jammie (she'd called me that since she was a baby). 'They said I talked weird. I don't know why … they're the ones that sound funny.' She blew her nose again. 'Then a girl said that people who go against the school uniform rules and wear jewellery are just trying to get attention. Were they talking about you?'

I shrugged; it was possible. I knew that to have something extra on your face just to make a statement when it wasn't your culture could be pretty dumb. Instantly, I felt a prickling behind my eyes. Was that why the girls were so unfriendly, why they seemed to look strangely at me? Did they think I had something to prove? I think I could take it if people didn't like me because I was different, but to be misunderstood? Now that was the pits!

Elly was staring at me. 'Since we're pretty abnormal right now,' I said, 'I think I'd feel sorry for anyone if they felt like this.'

'I hate this school.' Elly sniffed. 'I wish we could go back to Pakistan. There's no one here like Mary Jane.'

'You know we can't. Just give yourself more time.' I sounded just like Mum when all I wanted was someone to say it to me. 'It's only the first day.'

Mum had said that Elly would adjust the quickest since she was the youngest. Maybe she just needed something to cheer her up. 'Look, I'll take you down to the shops. Would you like that?'

Her eyes grew rounder than Basil's when I put his food bowl down. 'Yeah!'

We'd all liked shopping in Pakistan with its sense-enriching effect of sight, sound, smell and touch. Looking back on it now, it was always such a total experience—like Central Market and the Adelaide Show rolled into one—where everyone knew us.

Parabanks Shopping Centre was nothing like it. All look and no touch, rows of shelves and merchandise with no one saying, 'Come in and buy, have a cup of tea while you choose.' No haggling over the price of shoelaces. I bought Elly an ice-cream at Wendy's. It said three dollars seventy on the board and I asked if three dollars would do. The girl behind the counter got upset over that and I made a mental note not to do it again.

It was just after that when Elly saw the Teddy Bear Shop. At first it was fun—we looked at all the bears in the window, saying things like, 'I'll have that one!', 'No, that one's better', 'I'd call that one "Pooh" if he were mine.' All the normal things I presume people say in front of a teddy bear store window. Then we went inside. Elly picked up a little bear. 'I like this one,' she said. Then she ran to another. 'No, this one's more fluffy.'

Suddenly, I didn't know what she was doing. It had all

been a game before. But now? Did she think I was going to buy her a bear? They weren't cheap. 'Elly! Calm down.' I hurried over and there we were, surrounded by hundreds of bears, all cute, all gorgeous, all lovable and all too expensive. Elly looked weird and I was growing worried when all of a sudden she began to howl. Not just normal tears, but gut-shuddering, sobbing-type howling. The sort that you need to be out in the woods for. I held her tight right in the middle of the shop. It must have looked like some little kid having a tantrum because she couldn't have a bear, but Elly's not like that.

'There are so many,' she sobbed into my new T-shirt. 'They're so beautiful, but there's too … too many.'

I knew then what had happened in her little head and felt so sorry. Sorry that her brain couldn't compute a hundred bears at once, sorry that she'd never seen a shop like it before, sorry that she had to feel something was wrong because she was unable to cope with the hugeness of it all.

'Come on, sissie.' I finally steered her out of the store. 'Let's go home for supper.' We still called dinner 'supper' at that point.

By the time we arrived home, Elly was more herself and was able to tell Dad about 'all the bears'. Mum had on that crinkled forehead look of hers, which told me something was up.

'A phone call came for you, Jaime. The principal wants to see you in her office first thing in the morning.' Mum's eyes flickered to my nose pin. My thoughts had led up the same track. Still, Mum and I had already talked about what we might do if too much was made of the pin.

Dear Pakistan

I can't begin to tell you what a **** (Dad would kill me if he found me writing swear words) day it's been so I won't. I don't feel like thinking about it, so I'll think about you instead.

Right now we'd be home for holidays and it'd be snowing in Abbottabad (everyone here thinks all of Pakistan is hot—they don't know a thing) and we'd be making snowballs and throwing them at Dad. He used to be so much fun. I can tell he misses you too, he's so quiet, it's weird. Then we'd be going in to sit by the wood fire and Dad'd tell jokes. Maybe Shuhilla would make us chapattis and chai—she made the best tea, all milky and sweet. Oh God, take me back. How could we have left?

Jameela

P.S. I bet they're going to try and get my nose pin off me but they won't. It's the only physical part of me that I've got of you—the only thing to help me remember who I really am.

3

The principal didn't seem a bad sort really. She was making conversation about her nieces and nephews who went to school in Indonesia because their parents worked there. All the time, I carefully kept the left side of my nose facing the wall. I must have looked odd sitting with my head on a slant like that, but while the conversation was relatively safe, I wasn't taking any chances.

It wasn't long before I realised that Mrs Whitehead's topic wasn't safe at all.

'I quite understand about children being brought up in a different culture from their own. My niece writes me regularly and I've visited there. That's a Muslim environment too.' I pursed my lips, imagining what was coming next.

'They have quite a few different customs in Indonesia.' Mrs Whitehead fumbled for her pen on the desk. 'The girls wear scarves on their heads to school and they're not allowed to talk to boys.' It sure sounded like Pakistan.

'But,' the principal's tone changed slightly, 'they do those things because they try to fit into the culture there.' The slight emphasis on the word 'there' wasn't wasted on me. 'Wherever people find themselves they should try and fit in and respect the rules of the place where they are living.' Her mouth widened into a smile. 'Like, when in Rome do as the Romans do?'

I think she expected me to say something then, but I wasn't much help. Finally, my fears were founded. 'For example, girls here don't wear scarves to school, so we wouldn't expect you to, even though you've been brought up in a Muslim country.'

My tongue stirred into self-defence. 'But I saw an Indonesian girl in town on the weekend and she had a scarf on. Nobody was staring.'

By the look on the principal's face, I felt as if I'd played into her hands. 'Yes, my dear. But she was Indonesian and a Muslim.' I must have looked stubborn for she asked, 'Are you a Muslim, Jaime?' I shook my head.

'Then you wouldn't think of wearing a scarf here to school, would you?'

Basically, I agreed about the head coverings, but I had to hang on because I knew where it was all heading. Mrs Whitehead's voice got sweeter like Mum's, coaxing me to eat a spoonful of jam as a kid; we both knew it had crushed up, bitter tablets mixed in it.

'The nose pin doesn't bother me personally. I understand these things, but we have had complaints from certain parents.'

'But the nose pin is different!' I tried to follow the logic started by the scarves. 'The pin doesn't have a religious significance, sure, but it's cultural. It's about how I grew up. Every girl did it there. Why can't I keep it here?'

'It's about our rules now, Jaime. We don't wear nose pins or jewellery in this school. If you continue to wear it you may be misunderstood. Already some adults are referring to you in degrading terms because of it.'

'But, when they got to know me …'

'I'm sorry, Jaime. I didn't want to bring this up until you'd been with us for a few weeks. By then you may have seen for yourself that it wouldn't work. If I make an exception for you other students will expect special treatment also, and they may do it for the wrong reasons, not understanding yours.'

I could feel something wet making a wobbly track down my cheek. Already I sensed I'd argued too much. In Pakistan we were taught to respect authority. In national schools there, the high school students still stood whenever the teacher entered or left the room and no one would have dared to argue. No one had to; they all knew the same rules.

Mrs Whitehead watched me. To be fair, she looked kind, but she was waiting. I sensed that she wouldn't force me to take out the pin, but I could tell it was understood what had to be done. Gone was my resolve; I didn't feel strong enough. What if I kept it and still didn't know who I was? Suddenly I felt like getting in first; at least that way I was still in control of what happened to me.

'I understand your position, Mrs Whitehead. I'll … I'll take it out.'

It was almost worth it to see how surprised the principal looked. Then she smiled. 'What a mature thing to say. We could do with a few more with attitudes like yours.' She came round from behind the desk. 'Maybe you could put it back in after school, like pierced ears, and keep the hole open.' She truly sounded hopeful, as though she cared. I appreciated that, except it started me crying properly.

'Thanks.' I accepted the proffered tissue and managed to smile through my bleary eyes. It wasn't a real smile though for I knew Mrs Whitehead didn't know the first thing about nose pins. Noses heal up so much faster than ears; it would never work putting it in after school.

Dear Pakistan

I've heard about what people go through when someone dies. Well, that's what I feel like right now. Something's dying. I'm not sure if it's you or me. It feels like my heart is so sick, it's on a life support machine ... one flick and it'd be gone. Why doesn't God zap me back to you? My life was fine with you. I knew everything and what to do.

Mum isn't the type of person to make a fuss about the pin at school and Dad's not all here, if you know what I mean. Maybe this is what he's been feeling like but I can't help, can I, when I feel the same? Anyway, tomorrow I'll take the pin out. It was so much trouble getting it in, too. Mum asked me tonight if I'd rather they'd never given me permission to have it, but I said it had been worth it, even for a few years.

I guess what hurts is that I thought there was no discrimination here, but there is. I'm so confused. I have this feeling that if I'd said I was Muslim today, or if I was brown, I might have been able to keep the nose pin. I feel brown on the inside.

Can't anyone besides you see that?

Jameela

4

School became less depressing once I'd met Danny. He was kind. All I needed was a friend to talk to and, looking back on it, he may not have understood that, but he did get me through those first few months.

Danny was in Year 12, dark and good-looking. That might sound typical but dark good looks don't do much for me; in Pakistan everyone is dark and reasonably good-looking. Some of the girls in my class (especially Kate Sample) said he was 'hot', but wouldn't go out with him for reasons I could find out for myself.

His first comment to me sort of took my breath away.

'Hey, why did you take your nose thing out? I thought it was cool. You looked just like an Indian princess.'

I decided then that he could be my friend for life. He was totally sympathetic about it all and listened for ages. Nor did he ever seem to mind me talking about Pakistan. So far he was the only one I'd had an intelligent conversation with about my past life. It felt so good. Soon I looked forward to lunches.

'Where will we eat this time?' he'd say. 'Oval or lawn?' He had a group of friends, girls included, and I joined them.

The girls in my class picked on me for sitting with Year 12s. I was amazed that they couldn't hear how immature they sounded.

We didn't always talk about Pakistan. I found there was a lot I still didn't know about Australia. Mum and Dad had done their best to bring us up as Australians in a host country, but the first time Danny asked me if I wanted a pie or a pasty, I found myself wishing Mum had been more thorough. I thought it was best to come clean. 'What's a pasty?'

He grinned and ran off to the canteen, calling back, 'I'll show you.' I think he enjoyed showing me stuff.

One weekend I went to his house for tea. I'd decided to keep our relationship platonic; I didn't think I could cope with anything else at the time and he seemed happy enough. Besides, there was Suneel, though deep down I knew that was just a dream. Danny's family was great. It was just like being in Pakistan (well, almost). His mum and dad were loud and happy. He had numerous brothers and sisters, and cousins that kept dropping in through the evening. Even their home was decorated like houses in Pakistan: quite bright, with a lot of ornaments like clocks and vases that were not really for use.

Even though Danny's relatives spoke Greek among themselves I still felt at home. He apologised at one point but I assured him, 'Don't worry. In Pakistan there was so much I didn't understand, people spoke their local languages at home. I'm enjoying it.'

He leaned closer. 'It's good to see you happy, Jaime.' I

wondered if I always looked depressed at school. I'd have to work on that.

Just then, his mother called to him from across the room. I'd noticed she was the only one he spoke Greek to the whole evening but he didn't answer her this time. She nudged her husband and laughed.

'What did she say?' I noticed that Danny wasn't smiling any more. I wondered what the joke could be if he didn't like it. 'Was it about me?'

His little sister came to my rescue (if you could call it that). 'Mama said she didn't know there were Australian girls as nice as Greek girls. She doesn't mind Danny having an Australian girlfriend now.'

I glanced across at Danny. He still didn't comment. Instantly I was confused again. Did that mean he wanted me for a girlfriend or any Australian girl? Did that mean he didn't like Greek girls? Why? One thing was obvious: he wasn't about to say anything with all his relatives watching every move we both made, so I kept my mouth shut until later.

Later came earlier than I expected, in the car outside our house when he tried to kiss me. For a start, I didn't want to be kissed. Looking back now, there's no way I could explain that; I just didn't want our relationship to change, I guess. Once you make a boyfriend out of a guy, you can lose him. A friend you never lose if you don't want to.

There was something else too, a feeling, which was beginning to rise up and almost suffocate me like a huge black rug. I was terrified of being in the car out in the street where I could be seen. Wouldn't I get a bad name? From what the girls said at school, no one had a bad name now in Australia because nothing was wrong anymore, but deep down I didn't believe them. In Pakistan, girls were beaten for less than I was doing now, and boys killed for sleeping with a girl, if they got caught.

What was I thinking? Danny wasn't like that. He just wanted a kiss. The moment passed. As it was, he hadn't been desperate for one, just thought it was the thing to do.

'I'm sorry, Jaime. I didn't mean to come on like that. I only wanted to show you that I thought you were cool.' He sounded genuinely hurt. I tried to remember if I'd physically pushed him away.

'I wasn't upset. It's just ... where I was brought up—' it all came flashing back '—we couldn't do anything like this there.' I giggled, knowing nothing was funny. Credit must go to Danny, though, for he didn't say anything nasty, just gave me a hug. I still found that uncomfortable. I could imagine all the neighbours looking out their darkened rooms, peering at me through the curtains. I needn't have worried. I'd forgotten how Australian neighbours weren't too interested in what you do.

All of a sudden I felt sorry for Danny. A vision of Kate Sample passed through my mind. By the way she raved on at school, she wouldn't be acting like this with a guy. I could just imagine the girls' incredulous cackles and snide comments if ever they found out. Maybe it was to appease my conscience as well as to make it up to Danny that I invited him in for coffee. Dad had recently bought some excellent beans—it was one of the few things he'd missed from here while we were in Pakistan.

Danny was quick to accept. 'The night's still young,' he said with a grin. Did I detect a note of relief as well? Mum and Dad were still up. Mum was watching TV but Dad was reading. He still couldn't stand Australian media—too raw, he'd say.

I guided Danny through to the kitchen. I wanted him to myself to ask him a question. I settled him on the stool and came straight out with it while I got out the mugs. 'Danny, would you say you were Greek?'

Gone was his easy smile. He looked ready to go home and for a moment I thought he wouldn't answer. But he must have thought I needed to know.

'No, I'm Australian.'

'Why do you say that?' He started to answer but I wanted him to understand my motives. 'I'm not having a go at you, I just want to work something out, that's all.'

'Look, it's simple. My parents were born in Greece. They still call themselves Greek—well, most of the time. I was born here. That makes me Australian.'

'But why did your mum say that about Greek girls?'

'Because she wants me to be Greek and the only way she understands to keep people in the same old ways is to marry the same old ways. She's got a few Greek girls lined up that have been "brought up properly".' He grinned, finally. 'Terribly orthodox—can't think for themselves. I want to marry who I like—Australian or Greek. I don't need to keep all the old ways. Maybe I will when I'm forty.'

I digested all that. He looked Greek, yet everything he did and said denied what he was. And what if he decided that I was orthodox and couldn't think? Was that his criterion, or did it matter most not to be Greek?

'What about you? It's your turn. Are you Pakistani?'

'N–No …' Just then the kettle boiled. I spent the next few minutes with my back to him trying to sort out my thoughts. I hadn't expected him to ask me in return.

'Why not?'

'Because I was brought up Australian. I was born here, my parents are Australian. Even though I did most things in the Pakistani way, I knew I wasn't Pakistani.'

'Then what's your problem?'

How perceptive he was or did my confusion show so very much?

'Now I'm here, I'm not so sure anymore. It was easy in Pakistan. Being Australian meant having a different religion, speaking with an accent, knowing about cricket, showing pictures of kangaroos and the outback. It was obvious I wasn't Pakistani, even though I dressed like one, did things the same, had Pakistani friends and got a nose pin.'

'And here?'

'Now I don't know what "Australian" is any more. I'm not the same as anyone here—I might look like the kids at school but I think differently. It's like I came out of a round shape, got changed to an oval one, and now I've come back, I don't fit. Look at you, I would have called you Greek. You look Greek, but you're Australian. Just being born here can't do it, surely?'

Danny didn't answer. Maybe he didn't know how or hadn't thought about it much; he'd been so busy concentrating on being like the other kids. Maybe he'd never consciously followed a plan. Perhaps it just happened. Part of me wished it would happen to me. The in-betweenness was getting to me. Yet I knew too that I didn't want to be a duplicate of everyone else. Surely that wouldn't be me.

Almost as though he'd followed my thoughts, Danny came in with: 'You have to give yourself time. Why do you have to change anyway? I like you the way you are.' He grinned before he added, 'Sort of old-worldish Greek, but Australian all the same.' That was the first time I wondered if it would be easy to love Danny. He certainly said the nicest things. At that time I guess it was what I needed; every hug or bit of attention made me feel like a balloon gradually being blown up again after it had been let loose.

I didn't want those thoughts to show, not yet, so I told him to drink his coffee, but his dark eyes met mine over his mug. I didn't meet his gaze for long—old habits are hard to break.

Dear Pakistan

Drinking coffee with Danny tonight made me wonder about Suneel. Not that there's anything to wonder about. Mum said nothing could come of it and I know she's right. Mr Bolden gave us a huge English assignment yesterday that's supposed to span the semester and we're meant to add to it continually like a journal. It sounded so boring. Day-to-day stuff always is. I'll hand up what I write to you in this journal but I'll also make up an adventure. About Suneel. Then it'll be bearable to write. So what if none of it happened? I'll pretend it did.

It could start that day I saw him in the goat field. That bit was true at least.

Once upon a time in a faraway land of hot shimmering sands and high mountain peaks (what a paradox you are, dear Pakistan) there lived a young goat herder. His name was Suneel. He looked as though he didn't belong there, standing on the mountain slope, staring out to the snowy peaks in the distance. Even from the road, I could see there was something about him that set him apart.

It wasn't just that he was fairer than the average Pakistani (Alexander children they call the fair Northerners, after Alexander the Great). Nor was it the scar that ran down his right cheek, but an aura about him as if there were secrets he never told.

Maybe he didn't even know.

5

At school on Monday, I thought I'd ask Kate Sample and Debra what they'd meant about Danny. It had got around that I'd gone to his place on the weekend. I'd found another similarity to Pakistan: everyone knew everyone else's business there too. Actually, Kate brought it up herself.

'I hear you went to Danny's house.' No 'Oh, how nice, did you have a good time?', but 'I hear you went'.

'So?' I must have looked annoyed for she explained herself.

'I'm just trying to help because you're new. You know, it wouldn't do to get too involved with him.'

I bristled, more with curiosity than annoyance at that point. What on earth was she about to say? She sounded like some old-fashioned nursemaid in an ancient movie and the image didn't suit her at all.

'Why? Is there a problem?'

'Of course. I'm not racist at all, but he is Greek and you're not.'

I almost said her perceptual prowess was rather good, but thought better of making an enemy of her. 'What's that got to do with being friends?' I said instead.

'Being friends is fine, I guess, but they have different ways. Coming from another country you mightn't understand.'

Now since I knew Danny was more Australian than I was at that point, for her to talk like that to me sounded so prejudiced when she was only going by what I looked like. And I told her so.

'Kate, I can't believe you just said that. I thought Australia had anti-discrimination laws. I was told this is a multicultural country.'

She was a bit taken aback but she didn't let up. 'That's just for work and stuff. You know, same amount of work, same pay, no preference for jobs or bullying. That's only on the surface. Antidiscrimination laws can't tell you to be friends with people that you have nothing in common with.'

'But Danny's Australian.' Good thing I'd worked that one out for myself on the weekend.

'That's what he thinks. He's New Australian. There's a difference.'

I felt stubborn on Danny's behalf. 'He doesn't think so.'

Kate just stared at me then. It was strange. She actually looked sympathetic at first, then it changed to the frustrated way you'd look at a lamb that didn't need to be slaughtered but had followed the others up the ramp anyway.

'If you must know, Jaime, it's because of that he's always so determined to get an Anglo girl—any Anglo girl. One day, he'll have to marry someone his family picks out and in the meantime, he'll do it with as many girls as he can.

He's just using you. You should get interested in boys like Blake Townsend. His family won't be arranging a marriage for him.'

She practically flounced off to join Debra while I tried to find Danny. I was more confused than ever. No rules on the surface but there were some, after all. I didn't believe a word of what Kate said about Danny. I mean, it could have been true that he wanted an Australian girl, and I understood that, but I didn't agree with her reasons. Danny would never use me; we were friends.

I didn't manage to talk to Danny about it that day. He was on the court playing basketball most of lunchtime. Maybe he thought, since he could see me on the weekends, we wouldn't need to spend so much time together at school. It hurt a bit, as without meaning to, I kept remembering Kate's words, and I couldn't help wondering if Danny was disappointed with me in some way.

All the way home I worried over it in my mind like a pup with an old slipper and was totally unprepared when I opened our side door. My brother was crying! It was a sound I hadn't heard in years, not since he fell off a tonga—a horse-drawn cab—when he was ten. I rushed in, my own problems forgotten. He was sitting on the stool in the middle of the kitchen with Mum on her haunches dabbing Dettol on his legs. His left eye looked as if a rotten avocado had been pushed into it.

'What happened?'

Andrew stopped sobbing instantly. I wish guys wouldn't do that; they think only their mothers can ever hear them cry. Mum answered for him; she looked a bit tear-stained herself. 'He was beaten up.'

I raised my eyebrows at Andrew, expecting an explanation. I mean, he's so quiet! How could he ever get into a fight? It was definitely a first for the Richards' household. Andrew ignored me. He'd obviously said to Mum all he was going to say—bet that wasn't much, either.

'He wouldn't give up his Nikes.' Mum sighed. 'They took them anyway.'

'His sneakers? What sort of country is this? People aren't starving like they are in Pakistan and even they wouldn't beat up a kid for their shoes.' Take them when you weren't looking, but not fight you for them.

Andrew gave me one of those smiles as though nothing's funny but it's better than crying again. 'This isn't Pakistan, Jaime. Anyway it wasn't the shoes. They said they'd get me for having everything right all the time and because I talked weird.'

Even Mum looked surprised at this long speech. 'So it was kids from school then?'

'Only one, and he didn't do anything—tried to stop them.

He had his friends with him from another school.'

'He must have told them about you,' Mum murmured.

I was speechless; not a common occurrence. Andrew and I had bought Nikes in Singapore on the way home. We didn't understand how special they were at the time. Now, at the price they were in Australia, we'd never be able to replace them. Dad still didn't have a job. I stood there staring at Andrew.

Did he feel like I was beginning to feel? Maybe worse—that we weren't safe anymore? Good grief, kids that beat you up because you worked hard at school! Andrew was a perfectionist but why should it bother anyone else? I hadn't admitted it to anyone, but sometimes even walking down the street here I could feel strange, especially if someone came toward me with an off-the-planet hairstyle or wore clothes I wasn't used to. I'd feel like shrinking into the next shopfront.

Now I imagined Mum not letting us out. I didn't feel like helping, so I went outside to find Elly. Her uncomplicated way of looking at life could be refreshing at times. She was sailing paper creations on the fishpond, while Basil looked on with a still-life, interested set to his ears. I watched her for a moment. She looked so peaceful; life seemed simpler when I was around her. My eyes got all misted up then. What if something happened to Elly?

That was when I made a snap decision, something Dad used to be able to do. He used to say in Pakistan that if you were scared of anything, meet it head on, then it won't seem so bad. It seemed strange to think of Dad saying that now, but he took enormous risks when we were in Pakistan. He was even jailed overnight for lighting fire crackers. How was he to know no loud noises were allowed at election time? Yet he always came through and was ready for the next adventure. And he wasn't the only one: I'd had adventures too.

'Elly, do you want to go down the street again?' Sure, I

was scared, but I kept seeing Dad as he used to be. I didn't want to be like he was now.

Elly's eyes were wary. 'Do you think it's OK, Jammie?'

'You saw Andrew, did you?' She nodded.

'Then we'll ask Mum.'

Mum wasn't pleased but I think her head was too full of whether she should take Andrew to the doctor to worry about us right then. And lightning never strikes twice in the same place, I reminded her.

'Only be an hour,' she said. For once her 'cool' was ruffled. That was how I understood 'cool'.

We didn't go near the Teddy Bear Shop this time. I'm not that much of a fear-facer. But we had a thickshake at Wendy's. I didn't ask for it cheaper and we sat on one of those garden-like benches in the mall, both sipping it at the same time through thick pink straws.

As we sat there, Elly contentedly slurping, I watched the people, some taking their time, others hurrying as if a deadline depended on it. In Pakistan, no one hurried. It was rude to rush or show emotion of any kind, especially for a girl, as it was thought to draw attention. No respectable girl drew attention to herself in Pakistan.

I was idly thinking how many types of jeans there were and that just the act of wearing them didn't mean you had the right ones on. I knew I was wearing the wrong ones. But I decided not to be too concerned. What could I do anyway? They could stuff their cool labels. What did it matter? Did the best jeans get the best guys, the best marks at school, a place in heaven? Some girls at school, Debra for instance, acted as though Levi jeans saved your soul.

Just then I saw a flash of bright, flowing material. It looked so out-of-place among all the blue jeans and black shorts and T-shirts. I stood up to get a better look, and sure enough, there was a Middle-Eastern-looking girl, with long dark hair to the shoulders, baggy pants and long top, a scarf fluttering a little as she made her way down the mall. It only took a second to act.

'Stay here, Elly. I'll be right back.' I forgot all my training and ran down the path after the girl as if my life depended on it.

'Excuse me ...'

What if she'd become so Australian she ignored me? She'd most probably been told not to talk to strangers. She stopped, surprise making her mouth open slightly. At that moment, she reminded me so much of Ayesha, I could hardly speak. I tried to smile reassuringly. 'Excuse me, but are you from Pakistan or India?' She looked Pakistani but one had to be sure. Indians could get upset being taken for Pakistanis and vice versa.

Her voice was pure music: 'I am from Pakistan, ji. Why do you ask?' I was so glad I had a long top on over my jeans. I had been toying with the idea of trying on a skirt before we went but I still couldn't find the courage for that.

'I've lived in Pakistan most of my life. It's so lovely to meet you.' I couldn't go on. It really did feel so good that tears were welling in my eyes; that aching sensation started up behind my throat. I felt embarrassed and she turned her head away as if she knew. Then I asked her for what my mother had told me not to give if anyone asked me.

'Could you give me your phone number and may I ring you? Maybe we could meet?'

She actually smiled and said ji. But Easterners are like that, not as private as Australians. She wrote a number on a piece of paper from her bag. 'And yours?'

'Of course.' And would you know it, I couldn't remember the last two numbers. 'I'm sorry, we haven't been back long. I'm still not used to everything.' I gave up on that line of thought. 'My name is Jaime.'

'Mine is Yasmeen. What did they call you in Pakistan?'

'Jameela.' Oh, someone at last who understood where I'd come from! Even Danny didn't know about my other name.

'What a beautiful name for a beautiful girl.'

I grinned. I knew it was the Eastern way to be polite. Besides, just being white in Pakistan got me called beautiful. It wouldn't have mattered if I had a huge conk for a nose or cauliflower ears. It was being fair that mattered there.

I practically floated home on a cloud. Nor could I remember a thing that Elly chattered on about. Mum was pleased for me. It's a hard sensation to describe. I suddenly realised that I'd been feeling so down because everything I knew had been left behind. It had been like looking out a window into a dark landscape. Now, I'd seen a glimmer of light—as if I'd found a bit of Pakistan here—the 'something familiar' I'd been trying to find that Mum had said not to look for. God was good. He'd sent me Yasmeen. Mum went on about there never being Pakistanis living in Salisbury;

they usually settled in the Eastern suburbs. I was barely listening. All I could think about was seeing Yasmeen again!

Dear Pakistan,
I haven't time to write much. You don't mind do you? There are four assignments due in a couple of days and three of them are for external assessment. So they have to be good. Meeting Yasmeen has put an entirely new perspective on things. Schoolwork pales into insignificance, so does Danny even. I've got much more feel for my English assignment:

There were only five days until election time. The bazaar in Chitral was no different from any other and as I walked down with my father peering into the little lean-to shops and dingy stalls, I could sense a tension in the small groups of men discussing and gesticulating together. My father could be embarrassing when he'd talk with the men and forget I was with him. He got that excited glint in his eye and I began to panic, as we were too far away from the hotel for me to respectably walk back by myself. Women must have a male relative with them in remote mountain places.

'So you think a new government can make a change?' He started in with Urdu to the group of men close by. They stopped in surprise for only a moment, then continued their argument, my father included.

I looked around for something to take my attention; it was immodest to show interest in the men's conversation. That was when I noticed him, the same guy I saw in the goat field the day before.

He was buying something in a rug shop behind me. I could hear him talking to the shopkeeper, haggling over the price of a piece of tribal jewellery. He spoke in the way of the educated, using the national language, Urdu, with an English word scattered here and there. I used to think the rich did this to impress but from him it sounded so natural as if he didn't know the local tongue.

'Suneel,' the other man was saying in Chitrali. I lost the rest because I couldn't understand, but the young man broke in with, 'Old man' (a respectful title in Pakistan). 'I know I'll never find another one to match it, but the price is too high.'

He walked out then, in the timeless fashion of bargaining. Unfortunately, I was in his way. He bumped into me and apologised profusely, holding his arm across his chest in abject humility. The shopkeeper was right behind him. I could tell he was badgering Suneel to buy. 'Nay,' Suneel replied. 'It is too expensive.' He walked past me. By the noise from the shopkeeper I could tell he was giving in. Suneel turned back and bought the item for a cheaper price than even Dad would have got it for.

Just then, Dad turned to me, also apologising for leaving me on the road, when he noticed Suneel emerging from the shop. My father had an insatiable desire to start conversations. In no time, we'd been invited to have afternoon tea at Suneel's house the following day. For once, I wasn't cross with Dad for stretching our social calendar to its limit. Close up, Suneel had looked even more interesting.

6

It was the weekend at last! Because of all the homework, I had to choose whether to see Danny or Yasmeen. I think it's only people who don't care about passing who have a social life in Years 11 and 12. Danny took it well and said, 'That's cool.' He had a lot of work to hand in on Monday anyway, and there I was, finally at Yasmeen's house dressed in one of my favourite shalwar qameezes.

She'd just opened the door, a teenage boy hovering behind her, and instantly I was seeing Suneel again, just as I saw him in the goat field. Except Suneel had brown hair and his eyes were green like the water off a tropical island in travel magazines, not dark like everyone else's. I'd often wondered about that.

Suddenly I realised I must have been staring. Yasmeen was giggling slightly in the way a Pakistani shows embarrassment.

'I'm sorry,' I murmured, hoping I wasn't turning pink. 'Your brother reminded me of someone.'

'He is handsome, is he not?' Yasmeen giggled again.

I half smiled to be polite, knowing it was better not to show too much interest. He came forward to meet me. Like all younger brothers, he'd probably been hanging around all afternoon waiting for a glimpse of his big sister's new friend. Yasmeen introduced us, 'This is Shehzad.'

Close up, I lost interest. He was nothing like Suneel. His eyes were dark brown and he had a little too much personality and looked as if he knew it. When he spoke, his voice startled me into looking up at him again. It sounded like it should have come from a blond, bronze surfie. Even Danny's accent wasn't quite so Australian.

Yasmeen soon whisked me off through the house to her room. Her mother had Bollywood songs playing and was cooking up a storm in the kitchen, making pakoras and shami kebabs for afternoon tea. It would have been easy to get embarrassed by all the trouble they went to for me if I hadn't been used to that easy hospitality in Pakistan.

In Yasmeen's room the first thing she did was take some material from her cupboard and say it was a gift. 'I bought it in Lahore,' she said proudly and I knew it was the best she had. She even offered to sew it into a shalwar qameez for me. I was so excited as at the time, when I couldn't work out what clothes would look good with what, I resorted to wearing the Pakistani national dress. I knew how to wear it and no one could say it didn't match or was the wrong label.

I loved the atmosphere of Yasmeen's house. The excitement I'd felt in local homes in Pakistan, visiting with my mother, I felt there with Yasmeen. Her mother greeted me in English, then spoke to Yasmeen in Urdu. She was impressed when I understood. Yasmeen told me her mother had no Australian friends despite their repeated efforts to offer the lady next door curries and Pakistani delicacies.

Yasmeen's father was a doctor at the government hospital. There was a younger sister too, Rosina, but Yasmeen didn't say much about her. Not long after we settled ourselves on the floor in Yasmeen's room, she asked me if I was a Muslim.

'No,' I replied simply, knowing this wouldn't offend her. 'I believe in one God though, like you.'

'Then there isn't much difference between us.' She looked pleased. I knew there was an ocean of difference, yet talking to her like that, I felt closer to her than I did to any of the Australian kids at school. Even Danny I'd never told I believed in God. Maybe it was private for a Westerner but a Muslim will always talk about it. It's their life, how they think and many of their daily customs are tied up in their beliefs.

'I'm so glad I met you,' I burst out suddenly. 'Australians are so different from Pakistanis.'

'But you are Australian,' she said gently. 'You are home.'

'I know.' I must have sounded miserable, for she looked sympathetic and moved closer. She was only a couple of years older than me, but just then, she seemed as wise and ancient as a tribal grandmother.

'Yasmeen, you wouldn't call yourself Australian, I suppose? Haven't taken out citizenship?'

She shook her head. 'I may not stay here. It has already been arranged that I will marry my cousin in Lahore. If he decides to come here to live, then I will return. Daddy still has property there and we send money back to our relatives.

Besides, I would never change my religion.'

At first I didn't see the connection between my question and her last statement until I remembered that in Pakistan, being Muslim was practically synonymous with being Pakistani. Pakistani Christians were rarely respected and to change from Islam was often seen to be the same as changing one's nationality, politics and identity. Changing one's faith there can be punishable by death.

I spoke tentatively, 'Here, you can believe what you want. At least I was told that.'

'Ji, one can. But we still have our system here. The mosque, our friends, the Pakistani community. The imam keeps a strict eye on us here just as they do in Pakistan.' Then she added hastily, 'This is good, of course. I want to be a good Muslim, to pray five times a day, study, be charitable, keep the fast.'

'What about Rosina?' I was interested in her. She was more my age. 'Does she think that too?'

Yasmeen took such a while in answering that I thought she'd ignored me until she shook her head. 'Nay, she finds it difficult to be a good Muslim. She rebels against my parents' wishes in dress, she won't speak Urdu with them, does not say her prayers or go to the mosque with us. I think she has friends at school that do not understand her—' (I could well believe it) '—and so to fit in she goes their way.'

Poor Yasmeen sounded weary as she continued, 'We can't have it both ways, it seems. I never had a close Australian friend but that was the sacrifice I had to make. You are the first Australian girl I've met who understands me. Even likes me?' This last was a question and I knew, without hearing, the hope and yearning behind it.

I grinned and reached over to hug her. 'Of course I do. You don't know what it's done for me to meet you. This is the happiest I've felt since I've come back.'

'But you're mistaken. I do know,' she answered. I bit back another grin. She'd taken my colloquial English literally.

The rest of the afternoon sped by with a sumptuous afternoon tea and reminiscences of Lahore in the winter and Murree, the Himalayan holiday resort, in the summer. It turned out we had been in both places at the same time on a few occasions but with all those millions, who'd have known?

Shehzad came out as I was saying goodbye. He'd been doing homework in his room, although, judging by the sounds of heavy metal that surged under the door, it was hard to imagine much work being done. Mrs Rasheed loaded me with salaams for all my family, glass bracelets from Lahore for Mum and Elly, and extra shami kebabs for Dad and Andrew.

'Ask your abu to come and visit my husband,' she urged. 'He gets home later.' I nodded, thinking how it might do Dad good.

'Catch ya later. It was cool meeting you,' Shehzad shot after me in his total Australian accent. Nothing like Yasmeen's. Was it that he was younger? Or did the religion make that much difference? He sure didn't look as if he was interested in mosques yet he still had that Pakistani politeness. He didn't try to shake my hand, nor did he look at me the way I'd seen some Australian boys do, as if they knew what colour bra I had on.

Dear Pakistan,
I felt like I was back with you today. Even Shehzad's Australian accent didn't spoil the effect; he still looked Pakistani. Yasmeen's invited me to her cousin's first birthday—a big deal, as you know.

Elly's watching Neighbours and Dad's been gruff and grumpy again with everyone, including Mum. He's sure changed. He used to be so much fun. Mum says it will pass and that we all have to be patient and not expect too much of ourselves and each other. I suppose I should talk to him, but I don't feel like asking him how he feels. I'm sure it'd be too depressing. Besides, my story about Suneel beckons me. Mr Bolden is one of those super-conscientious teachers. He wants to see weekly drafts.

Back at Dreamland Hotel ('Dreamland' was a definite overstatement but good old Mum had brought flea powder and clean sheets), I was telling Mum about Suneel, when Dad came in from talking to the proprietor.

'We can't stay as long as we thought. These little villages get rather hot at election times apparently. We've been advised to leave the valley.'

'When?' I held my breath. There was afternoon tea at Suneel's tomorrow.

Fortunately, Dad was never overly cautious. 'I

think the day after tomorrow will be time enough.'

I heaved a sigh of relief. He mistook the reason for it and ruffled my hair. 'Don't worry, sunshine. Things seem calm in the bazaar at the moment.'

I smiled up at him. I wasn't worried. He always had an uncanny knack of gauging an atmosphere so that he mostly kept out of trouble, getting into just enough to keep life exciting. How were we to know that this time he would misjudge the situation completely?

7

Danny was waiting for me when I arrived at school on Monday. I told him all about the Rasheeds. He seemed interested enough or maybe I was so full of myself that I didn't notice anything else. Except Kate, of course, as she and Debra walked past. Kate's eyebrows were perched so high they looked as if they'd fly right off her face. But I wasn't going to let her disapproval spoil my day. Besides, if all the girls thought like Kate, wouldn't Danny be in need of a friend?

All through maths, though, it wasn't Danny I was thinking of. I kept wondering what was going to happen in my story at Suneel's house. I mean, if he sounded educated and so must have been rich, how come he was in the goat field? I felt more secure in his world. I could imagine him understanding me like Yasmeen.

I couldn't help myself; I flipped over to the back of my graph exercise book and began writing furiously:

> Suneel's house was set back from the bazaar. We had to climb a small rise to reach the huge wrought iron gate. A button pushed on the outside obviously moved servants to action inside as within a few moments, we

were being ushered into a spacious central courtyard, the effect of which left vivid images on my mind: lush, rich, green, jungle. Cool-looking servants in white shalwar qameezes were bringing refreshments on trays as Suneel and an older woman came forward to greet us.

'Good afternoon. How pleasant to meet you,' she said in flawless English that sounded like a travel documentary. She was older than I'd expected Suneel's mother to be. As it turned out, she ...

'Jaime! What do you think you're doing? This is a maths lesson, not a time to catch up on homework.' Mr Williams' eyes under bristly black brows watched me all through the rest of the lesson; at least, I imagined they did. There was a hot spot right on top of my head.

I couldn't help what went on inside, though. Even in trigonometry, I used the measurements to work out how far Suneel's house was from the bazaar and at what angle one would need to leave his house to get to the river without being shot.

Lunchtime found me in the library. Danny had basketball practice, anyway. I suppose I could have gone to watch. Maybe I didn't try hard enough to be friends with the girls in my class but I didn't feel like hearing more of Kate's advice. All the girls around her seemed to think like her. Sara and her friends never went near me after that first day. There were others who I knew weren't my type who usually sniggered when I walked past.

I couldn't tell if it was my braids (no one else wore

them) or my school shoes, which I liked when Mum bought them but didn't know they weren't 'in' this year at school. I wondered who had decided they weren't 'in'. Someone like Debra, I guessed. Things like that didn't matter in Pakistan. Most people were glad to have shoes at all and I'd had the best ones anyway. Mum's Pakistani friends would hope Mum thought of them whenever I grew out of my clothes.

The quietest spot in the library was in the back corner, still in full view of the librarian and some other tables, but quiet enough not to be bothered. Wrong. I'd just started on the afternoon tea conversation at Suneel's. He'd actually sat down with us (under Elly's adoring gaze; I hoped mine was more controlled) and he hadn't whisked Dad and Andrew off to the men's quarters as so often happened in Pakistani households, when a shadow fell across my page.

'Hi! Jaime, isn't it?'

I looked up and froze. It was so unlike me and even now I can't explain it. The owner of the voice was Blake Townsend.

'You don't mind?' He pulled out a chair, knowing I wouldn't object. He had the confidence that came from never having been refused anything. I bet his mother gave him orange juice in his cot if he even whimpered. Blake Townsend was the major topic of all Kate's conversations. Even if she were talking about the weather, it got around to Blake somehow: 'Blake'd look really hot in a Bonds muscle top on a day like this.'

'So weren't you a princess in some remote country?' His

tone made him sound interested but I knew it wouldn't last long. Danny had made me feel warm with those same words. Now I just felt scared. It must have been because Blake was blond. I wasn't used to blond. He was also big, with one of those square jaws you only read about, and he was brown because he wanted to be, not because he was born with it and couldn't do anything about it. Besides all that, he was too close. For the first time I wished I hadn't worn braids that day. I wished my dress was a bit shorter. I wished I could say something smart.

'I always make it my business to meet new students. Sorry I'm a bit late.' I was wondering why he said that when my glance took in the student council badge on his blazer. It was his second time in Year 12; that probably made him the head rep in the school. He couldn't be too bad if everyone had voted for him.

I tried to smile as if I were relaxed. 'You took me by surprise,

I was engrossed.' I pointed to my book as explanation. He leaned forward as though to read it but I didn't hand it over.

'You like writing?'

I nodded. 'It makes me feel better.'

His eyebrows rose in surprise. 'Why should you need to feel better? You look like you've got it together.'

It was my turn to be surprised. Even Danny hadn't come out with something like that. 'What do you mean?' I was starting to feel a bit warm. I hoped it didn't show.

'Well, you're different and it seems like you don't mind

being different. Most of the girls at school are trying to be like someone in the media whether it suits them or not.'

That was laughable, when he looked exactly like he'd stepped out of a Coke ad. Maybe it was natural for him though. Most probably he was born looking like that so why should anyone else resent it? Maybe it's only trying to be something other than yourself that's wrong. I decided to come clean about the media bit.

'I never grew up with the Australian media. That's why it has no hold over me. I don't understand it. So, you see, I'm not really special at all. And I'm not a princess.'

He looked as though he was going to answer when our attention was taken by a nearby group of noisy kids banging their bags down and pulling out chairs. A guy called to Blake amid the librarian's inadequate shushes. That was when I noticed the glances thrown my way. I steeled myself for the usual amused smirk and held my breath waiting for Blake to disappear in embarrassment, but it didn't happen. The guys stared at me appreciatively, as if I were a pizza with the lot. The girls' glances were definitely envious.

I suddenly realised what Kate was on about. I hadn't seen it before, not when I was with Danny. Did being seen with Blake make so much difference? Why should it? He didn't even seem aware of the effect he was having. I'd seen both sides. He'd only ever seen one, I bet. He'd always received admiring glances so he wouldn't know what it was like not to have them.

Blake did leave after a while, but he left me feeling more confused than before. If he thought I was OK because

I was different, why did I only get the respect from the kids when I was with him? Could he accept me because he was older and saw through all that peer pressure stuff Mum used to talk about? Did that mean only older guys would appreciate me? Or maybe guys like Danny, brought up in a different cultural background, who didn't know the 'right' way of doing things? Did it matter? Surely not everyone was part of the 'in' group.

I felt as if I was in a lonely hole again. And it wasn't exactly a topic I could talk to Danny about.

Dear Pakistan,

I got an anonymous note today. It read, 'You're cool, Jaime Richards, but you can do better than Danny Dimitriadis'. I knew it wouldn't have been Blake's work. It didn't seem his style. I was so annoyed. I mean, who says I'm going out with Danny anyway? You only have to spend time with a guy here and everyone thinks you're 'together' (that's the word for it at school). But I guess it doesn't do to tell you all this. You wouldn't understand anyway; you most probably think I'm immoral, believing in arranged marriages as you do.

Besides it's too hard to work out so I won't think about it anymore. It's much more fun being at Suneel's.

After the refreshments, the servants had brought sweet, milky tea just like Shuhilla used to make at home on holidays. Elly had just started on the pakoras and samosas (simultaneously) when we heard the rata-tat of an assault rifle. Gunshots were often heard but not like this with sounds of jeep tyres squealing and engines being revved up, interspersed with shouts of anger.

Just as Suneel and his father rose there was a banging on the gate and a man almost fell into the courtyard.

'Sahib, Sahib ...' I didn't understand the garbled story of the distraught man but Suneel's tense face as he slipped the man some money gave me an idea of the importance of the situation. Even then, I was more excited than scared. With a quick apology flung back at us, Suneel's father stalked outside, shouting orders and testing the safety catch on the rifle a servant had handed to him. Men appeared from every corner and ran down the alleyway ahead of him towards the bazaar.

Suneel turned back to us, smiling mechanically, the perfect host. I felt sorry for I could tell he'd rather be in the action with his father.

'What's wrong?' Dad asked. 'Can I help?' He half stood, looking hopeful.

'It will be all right now,' Suneel replied, his voice like ironed silk. 'A man has got into an argument over politics and decided to make his point plain. It happens sometimes.' He made his face smile but he didn't seem amused.

'My husband will see to it,' Suneel's mother broke in, her voice as smooth as her son's. 'He is the khan. They will stop fighting and do what he says.' The way they kept reassuring us should have warned me but

I didn't take in the danger of the situation. All I could think was that Suneel's father was the khan! I looked with renewed interest at Suneel. That made him a kind of prince.

My father was standing now. 'I think we had better leave.'

Suneel motioned him down. 'I'm sorry, sir, but until the riot is stopped you cannot go back to the hotel.' He glanced at Mum and the rest of us. 'Some of our people do not think carefully when their temper is up. They have no restraint.'

Dad sighed in equally ill-concealed restraint. He wanted to go and look, I could tell. I grinned at him. He and I were much alike.

Mum was wearing her worried frown. Dad always said she thought too much. She turned to Suneel's mother. 'Are you in politics? Does it involve you other than putting down a riot?'

The other woman smiled briefly. 'My husband stands for election in this area. But for many, the election is only about the government.'

'Do you support the new one?' Mum asked.

'Ji.'

'And many don't, do they?'

I'd noticed by the strained look on Andrew's face that he was following her argument and coming to some conclusion of his own.

Mum continued, 'Then the riot may not stay confined to the bazaar?'

Andrew nodded slightly to himself.

Suneel sat down then and spoke slowly, his

voice firm, like heavy-duty denim this time. 'Please do not worry. There will be no further trouble.'

I don't think any of us, even Elly, were fooled by the 'please'. It was not an appeal. Mum stayed quiet then, but pulled Elly closer to her, rocking her as one would a baby in a thunderstorm.

8

Danny had just selected another song on his iPod. Despite my life resolve of trying to accept people as they came, I was still impressed at how well set up he was. He had his own music system in his room. There was a 'spare room now TV theatre' for all the kids and he could take any food he wanted from the kitchen cupboards or fridge when he felt like it. Mum would kill Andrew if he didn't ask first.

I was even learning to notice the clothes he wore on the weekends. They were nice, and on the back pocket of his jeans was one of the labels Debra dropped into conversations.

It was Saturday afternoon. We'd decided I would take my homework to Danny's place to collaborate (Mrs Smith's word) on my history assignment. History had become an analysis of the cricket and the political state of Africa. Danny said he'd help, for though I'd murmured noises in the right places about cricket in Pakistan and knew a lot about Imran Khan (most girls in Pakistan still did), I was totally ignorant of the political side of things.

'Just listen to this first.' Danny came over as I was

getting my books organised and put a set of headphones over my ears.

I was totally unprepared for the rush of sound that swept all around me. It made me bend my head to the left as the drums began the beat; the bass definitely came in from the right. As the lyrics started I fully expected a singer to be hanging from the ceiling. I can't remember if I actually looked upwards. Danny was grinning, saying something. It was as if I were suspended in a bubble with only loud, pure sound. It made a feeling rise in my chest that I couldn't identify, nor could I control it. Suddenly I was sobbing; the music stopped, and Danny was holding me.

'Jaime, I'm so sorry. I wasn't laughing at you.'

It took a while but I managed to reassure him. 'It wasn't you. It was the music. I've never heard anything like it. My 'phones or earbuds don't sound like that.' Danny pulled the plug out of the 'phones socket and the sound filled the room.

'It's different now. Before, it was intense, like it was making me feel something whether I wanted to or not.'

'That's the 'phones. I just bought them. Awesome, hey?' I was still unnerved. He tried to explain.

'It's just like the movies—surround sound. Drums from one speaker, voices from the other. You know, sounds from offstage can even sound behind you …' He said it as though I knew what he was talking about. I had no idea.

'I've never been.'

He grinned a bit uncertainly as if he hadn't heard correctly. 'Pardon?'

'It's true. I've never been to the movies. Mum hasn't had time yet …'

'You've got to be kidding! I go all the time with the guys. We see everything.' He looked at his watch. 'Look, ring your mum. There's a movie on in an hour. We can just make it on the bus.'

It was too fast. 'What about this history assignment? What do you wear? Do I look all right?' I can't believe I said that last bit.

He bent down to peck me on the cheek. 'You need educating, babe. Don't worry about the history. We'll do it later. And you look great!' His glance flicked to my hair. I'd worn it down with the fringe curled like Debra's. Apparently these things work after all.

Fortunately, Mum had shown us how to use the bus. That sounds weird now, but then, if the ticket machine made strange noises or spat out my ticket, it would throw me into a panic. Bus drivers weren't always a lot of help. The last time I was on one with Dad we didn't know where to get off, except for the number of the stop. Dad asked the driver to tell us when it was stop eight. The driver smirked and answered, 'Sure, mate, it's the one after seven.' We felt so dumb but we just hadn't known how the system worked.

It was totally different being with Danny. He didn't even have to think about where to get off, just stood up suddenly and said, 'We're here.'

The shopping centre was huge with ground-to-sky glass and escalators everywhere. That was another thing, but I wasn't about to tell Danny. The only escalators I'd used were at international airports.

Danny walked right onto one without missing a beat in his rhythm. Fortunately, I was behind him and he didn't see the hesitation or my hand gripping the rail too tightly. Getting off was a worry. I tried to time it just right, so I wouldn't get my feet caught in those little teeth at the end, but I landed in Danny's arms instead. He looked pleased, but it was a little too public for me.

I was surprised at how many people were there but I guess eight movie houses showing different films at once would draw a crowd. When I recognised some kids from school, I wished Mum and Dad had had time to take us themselves; then I wouldn't look such a geek.

Danny seemed happy enough as he pocketed the tickets. He apologised for paying, which I thought weird. I'm glad he did for I hadn't come prepared, nor did I realise how expensive it was. Many times I would still find myself thinking in rupees.

We ended up at the latest action movie. On the way down the carpeted hall we were laughing about something when a couple passed us, engrossed in each other. The girl looked Pakistani but I knew she wasn't; she had short stylish hair and the latest type of skirt that split up the side. Besides, the guy with her was a blond Australian and obviously taken with her. I knew I didn't look at Danny the way she was staring at her boyfriend. Nor did I ever look long enough at Danny to notice if he cared that much about me. Scary stuff.

Danny settled me down with Maltesers and Coke—he

knew how to do things well—and the film began. From almost the first moment I was in agony of some form or another. The screen was too big, the sound so intense, that there was no way not to get involved. I forgot about the Maltesers, let Danny drink the Coke, and hung onto his left hand all the way through. When guns fired, I flinched and I even ducked for cover at a few places. I cried at the emotional bits (quietly) and even gasped when one of the guys was shot and he twitched with blood spurting everywhere. That bit was disgusting. It took great self-control not to bury my head in Danny's safe shirt.

Every now and then he'd check how I was doing but he didn't see the way I was pushing myself further into the seat.

'Well?' Danny queried after an hour-and-a-half's whirl through crime and justice. 'How was it? Would you do it again?' Maybe he did know how difficult it was, for his hand had a few red marks on it.

I should have said 'no'. 'Yes, I'd do it again.'

He grinned, kind of proudly. I tried to explain to him later that it was like a challenge, like going to the bazaar in Pakistan incognito after a terrorist attack, causing emotions to run high against Westerners. It was exhilarating, a feeling I'd missed.

The look on Danny's face said, 'how could a movie do all that?' but he let me go on about it all the way to his house until he finally finished it with, 'Well, you'll get more of that if you go out with me.'

I stopped to look at him, then. 'Are we going out, Danny?'

'What do you think?' he asked seriously. Why did he do that—make me think? Was it because he didn't want to make a mistake?

'Kids think we're going out because we're together a lot at school.'

'And you just went out with me to the movies.'

'That's different, isn't it?'

He nodded.

'It's all words, Danny. I don't know what they mean. Can we still spend time together, be friends, even go out together but not "go out", I mean, as a couple?' I sounded so dumb, and—horror!—if Kate was right, this would be his bowing-out point. I held my breath because I suddenly realised I needed Danny's friendship, his easy way of dealing with things. He could see a bigger picture than me and help me not to get too uptight, too serious about myself.

He gave that 'what are you worried about' grin of his. 'That's cool. I know where you're coming from, Jaime.'

'You do?' Even I wasn't sure.

'Yeah, don't worry. It doesn't matter what everyone else thinks as long as we know what we're doing. Right?'

'Right.' I just hoped that he and I both knew what we each thought the other knew. I wondered if that was how he'd survived the flak he must have received at times from some of the kids: not worrying about it since he knew he was doing OK. That was a new concept for me. In Pakistan, I had to worry about what impression I was giving. The rules were different and there were so many of them.

Since he was being decent about it all, I thought I'd

better explain. 'You see, where I come from, girls aren't even friends with boys. It's totally taboo. Even in the international school I went to, if we had a friendship with a guy—and many friendships became more than that—it had to be kept quiet, for most of the staff were Pakistani. They would never understand.'

'What about out of school?'

'If we went down to the bazaar, the boys had to act like brothers, nothing else. They couldn't even touch us or there could have been repercussions. One couple were found practically doing it in the boys' dorm. They were expelled on the spot. We were warned about it a lot, and girls could be put in prison for being immoral so that's why I'm still cautious.'

After letting me go on, Danny's comment floored me. I thought he mightn't understand. 'We're much the same.'

'Who?'

'A lot of Greek girls can't have boyfriends. Their parents would have a fit.' He grinned. 'I know a few who get out their windows at night though.'

I began to feel that confused feeling again. I had quite a few of those and was beginning to recognise them: ones that made me sad as though I'd lost something; ones that made me feel misplaced, angry or homesick for Pakistan. This was the angry one.

'What about you? You can have a girlfriend because you're a guy?'

He answered me patiently enough, or did he sound just a wee bit weary? 'I told you, I'm not Greek, so the rule doesn't apply to me. Same as you. You're not Pakistani, so you can have a boyfriend.'

I didn't want to talk about it anymore. At times I didn't feel the tiniest bit Australian. That afternoon, I thought I had some of it put together but I'd lost it again. I asked Danny to take me home. I even surprised myself and let him kiss me in the car. The awful thing was I didn't care whether he did or not. It didn't turn out to be what Kate would call a proper kiss, anyway. She always said a guy hadn't kissed you properly unless he could tell afterwards if you still had your tonsils. At times she sounded so gross.

Mum opened the front door as we walked up to the porch. I tried to remember how long we'd sat in the car when I noticed she had an 'I'm mad but I'll be polite' look on her face. I hadn't seen it for a long time.

'There's a friend here to see you, Jaime,' she started in a low tone, then, 'How could you take so long to come in?'

I knew what she meant but I was afraid Danny wouldn't.

However, I forgot his Greek upbringing. He stepped forward immediately. 'I'm so sorry, Mrs Richards. I should have rung about being late. As it was, Jaime was working out some of her feelings about living in Australia.'

Mum visibly softened. It was the exact thing to say to her. How could he have known? It was basically true and I couldn't see any of the total Aussie guys in my class saying something like that. They wouldn't even know what was at stake.

'That's quite all right, Danny.' She was all smiles. Even I had never got her to that point so fast. 'I'm sorry I can't ask you in this time but I'm sure we'll see you again soon. Why don't you and your family come for tea sometime?'

Wow, was Mum ready for that? Even I wasn't sure how many there were.

Danny winked at me as he turned to leave. It made me feel warm again.

'Come in quickly,' Mum murmured. I was beginning to wonder what all the fuss could be about, when I heard my name called.

'Salaam, Jameela.'

'Hello, Jaime.' It was Yasmeen, her parents, even Shehzad, but no Rosina. I panicked—just like Pakistanis to come unannounced. We were used to it in Pakistan but not here. What if they guessed a boy brought me home? Would they think I was an unfit friend for Yasmeen? A bad influence on Shehzad? I implored Mum with my eyes to think of something.

She already had. 'A friend of the family just brought Jaime back from their home. Here she is, at last.' Friend of the family—so that's what Danny was now. I grinned. Mr Rasheed was introduced; then he and Dad resumed talking. Apart from the shock of finding them there, just seeing that small glint in Dad's eye again made my own eyes water.

'I'm so glad you came,' I said impulsively to Yasmeen and her mother. And I meant it, truly meant it.

Through cups of tea, biscuits and cake (our suppers were never quite as good as theirs) the evening passed without further panic. Shehzad was supposed to be talking to Andrew but I caught his glance on me a few times. I hoped Shehzad didn't guess about Danny as it mattered a great deal to me to be accepted by their family.

Apart from my own family, I still didn't feel as if I could hold my own anywhere. Even with Danny, there were times when I wasn't sure what he expected or how to keep it all together.

At Suneel's place, the noise from the bazaar had escalated to what sounded like a small-scale war. Dad was pacing the floor by the time Suneel's father returned. Mum saw him first; she's not a screamer any more than I am, so her horrified gasp unnerved me for a moment. The khan was supported by two men and blood dripped down his arm.

His wife scurried around making the distressed sounds a buffalo makes over her sick calf. Suneel somehow managed to stay calm throughout the proceedings of getting his father in to bed. When he returned to us, Dad had made up his mind.

'I'm really sorry about your father, Suneel. I think it best that we leave you in peace now. Maybe you have someone who could take us to the airport?'

'I am afraid, Mr Richards, that there is only one flight a day and that has been taken up with flying the wounded to hospital.'

I let my mouth gape. The plane was small but even so, to take up the whole flight would mean about twenty men wounded more badly than his father.

'Actually, I have called for a jeep to come when night falls. The driver will take you out of the valley to the next major village. There you will be able to get a bus to Peshawar.'

Just then two men came in with our bags from the hotel. Suneel had thought of everything, it seemed.

With dusk came quietness in the bazaar and I almost wondered if we needed to go. Maybe it was all over. I watched Dad and Suneel talking in low tones. Dad had that buoyed-up, hyped look about him.

Suneel—it hit me then—I'd never see him again. Would it matter? Half of me knew it wouldn't. He was too different, a part of this scene, and I wasn't. But another voice inside me protested about how exciting he was. I could learn to live here, couldn't I? I chided myself for being so stupid. His marriage would already be arranged and it wouldn't be to some foreign girl on a family holiday who just stumbled into his life.

'A penny for them?'

I jumped. Mum was at my elbow, following my gaze.

Feeling sheepish, I only grinned.

'It wouldn't work, you know,' was all she said.

'I know.'

But a girl can dream, can't she?

9

We were all invited to Yasmeen's house for her cousin's birthday party. That's just the way Pakistanis do things: the whole family matters. I made the mistake of telling Kate and Debra where I was going. They're as nosy as Pakistanis can be except Pakistanis are only nosy to know you better or pass the time of day. I didn't trust Kate's nosiness.

'You're crazy! And you're going with your parents?' She almost managed to repeat what I'd said word for word. It was about her most intelligent comment all day. She even looked as if she wanted to come but I wasn't fooled. It was Debra who voiced what was probably on both their minds.

'You're not going to go all ethnic on us, are you?' She made 'ethnic' sound like a headhunting course. 'You live here now. You don't have to keep getting involved with them.'

'Yeah,' Kate joined in. 'Let them keep their extremist views.' Look who was talking! My thoughts must have shown, for she continued, her voice reminding me of the fairy story where lizards fell out of the nasty sister's voice instead of roses. 'Unless of course you think they're better than us.'

There was nothing I could say as I suddenly realised I did think Pakistanis were better. Mum says every national or cultural group has its own idiosyncrasies and a certain character with good and negative attributes but just then there didn't seem to be any comparison with the Rasheeds' gentle and hospitable ways. I knew I shouldn't think like that. I'd been taught not to look down on other cultural groups but here I was, despising my very own.

I was so flustered I just hurried off to the bus, imagining I could still hear Kate's cackles. They would have thought they got the better of me, but who cared?

Actually, I did care. What if everyone thought like Kate? There would be no place for me here. I could see the next two years of high school stretching into the distance like those pictures of the Nullarbor Plain, just endless misery, waiting until I could get back to Pakistan. That was when I heard the screech of tyres and an angry voice shouting, 'Get off the road, you bloody idiot.'

I managed to reach the edge of the road but it was too late when I realised I was on the wrong side to catch the bus home. I watched it pull away from the kerb and I did something I don't remember doing since I was little: I cried in public. Not like Elly did in the Teddy Bear Shop but it was just as embarrassing and I couldn't stop. Every time I'd sniff and get my face upright it'd come crumbling down again.

'Hey.'

I was feeling so sorry for myself that I didn't hear the car idling beside me. When I became aware of it, I started walking as if my house was close by, pretending the car wasn't there. That was the way I handled wild dogs in Pakistan. If I ignored them, they left me alone.

Gone were the sobs; this feeling was worse than anything wild dogs had ever conjured up. All the other kids had gone on the bus. What if I was abducted? From what I'd heard on the news, there were serial killers behind every bush!

The car followed me, slowly, insidiously; the passenger door was opening.

'Jaime.'

They don't usually know your name, do they?

'Hey, Jaime!' The voice was more insistent now. And familiar. I sneaked a look and saw blue. Wasn't that the blue car always parked in the Year 12 area? The door was open, the driver's hand on the front seat, the other on the wheel.

'C'mon, hop in. I'll take you home.'

I slid my bag in and then myself. I still wasn't sure it was a great idea. 'Why did you do that, Blake? Don't you know crawling cars scare the hell out of girls?'

'I'm sorry. You looked so miserable, all I could think of was helping.'

'Thanks, anyway.'

'You in a spot of trouble?' Was that part of his student council job, to check up on kids in distress?

I wasn't going to tell him anything at all but it all tumbled out amid directions to our house, even to being sworn at on the street. He was so much easier to talk to than any of the teachers. In a way it was even easier than talking to Danny for I was beginning to realise that Danny relied too much on my responses as if he had a personal stake in the outcome. Blake didn't.

'You know, I was born in the back of beyond.' He grinned as I stared across at him in surprise.

'You?'

'Yep. Beyond the proverbial black stump. I board with a family so I know a little of what it's like to be out of your environment.' His attention was taken for a moment, changing gears.

'Why does everyone have to be from another culture or a different environment to understand how I feel? Why?' I sounded bitter, even childish. Deep down, I knew the answer, even then.

'Because people are basically self-centred. We only know our own scene. We feel secure in that. Different ways, different people upset the equilibrium.'

I wouldn't have been that blunt but it sure gave me an open window into what he must have gone through in the beginning.

'You made it.' My voice was almost a whisper but he grinned.

'One day I realised I was thinking just like they were – why don't they see me, understand me? When you were in Pakistan, I bet you did things the way the people did there. Why?'

'Because they wouldn't understand anything else.'

'Same here. I had to put myself into these city kids' shoes.'

'But everyone here's educated. They know better. They

should be able to accept different people. In Pakistan only twenty-five percent of the people could read. Maybe only half the population understood there was even a world beyond the Middle East. They can't help the way they think.'

'It's not education that does it, I'm afraid.'

'But I don't want to be like the kids here, to think like them. It's so provincial, so … so rude and unfriendly. Their jokes aren't funny, just putting someone down.' I couldn't think of more things to say that adequately described what I felt right then. 'Besides, it's cold here when it rains.'

Blake's voice was surprisingly gentle. I thought he'd call me out for being discriminatory myself. 'You don't have to think like them. You never will. You'll always be that little bit weird, different.' He smiled and I liked it. He made weird sound special.

'But we have to understand how they think or why they do things and not step on toes. We have to show we're willing to listen, like we want them to listen to us.' He almost had me won over when he ruined it. 'We have to show we need them.'

'Need them? They've got nothing I need. Like a hole in the head I need them.'

'There must be something. I bet you can't pick out clothes yet.' How did he know? 'Couldn't you ask one of the girls to take you shopping?'

I bristled like Basil's tail when the dog next door puts his paws on the top of our fence. 'I don't care about having the right clothes on. They're stupid. The skirts are too short, the tops are too tight, the colours don't suit me.'

'That wouldn't stop the girls at school.' He actually laughed, then stopped when he saw I didn't even smile. 'OK. What about something else? Say you want to buy a present for someone, so you go to town to get it.'

'I don't know how to go to town. The trains scare me.'

'Then ask one of the girls to take you.'

But who? Kate didn't fit the description of a Good Samaritan and the image of Debra solicitously explaining how to buy a train ticket suddenly revived my sense of humour.

I glanced across at Blake who was concentrating on a corner. There were many things I didn't know. Mum hadn't had time to do everything, and besides, she had a fortyish way of picking out presents. I knew girls here would rather jewellery or a DVD than a cute box for the dressing table. How would I ever pick out a DVD? Grudgingly, I started to get his point.

'Is that what you did?'

'Yeah, my old man gave me some advice when I first came down to the city. He said, "Son, keep your mouth shut, don't think you're better and at the first opportunity, ask for help."'

'Did you do it?'

'Not at first. I was a real rookie. I still said "g'day" when everyone else said "hi". I couldn't hear the difference.' I looked at him in sympathy. I wasn't that bad.

'I'd never been to the movies,' he went on. I grinned. 'Got in with the wrong chick—nearly got into trouble.

I couldn't read the cues. It was like being on the freeway going the wrong way but the signs saying "go back" were in a foreign language.'

Tell me about it, I was thinking; I'd been there too. I still was. 'After a few scrapes on the oval, I remembered Dad's advice. It worked. That's why I'm passing it on to you. Maybe you could try it.'

He turned the engine off. It took a moment to realise we were home already. I just sat there, not knowing what to say. He'd made me feel better but how to say that without seeming to come on to him?

'Thanks,' was all I said. He smiled a bronze Aussie smile as he leaned over and opened the door. I found out later it didn't open for anyone else but him.

'Don't try too hard, Jaime. You'll do OK.' His voice actually wobbled a bit and I heard the raw faith as if he'd spelled it out for a hard-of-hearing person. He really meant it. One tear dribbled down my face as I quickly got out and ran up to the porch. I turned and waved. I was crying again but this time I didn't mind; someone actually believed I'd make it!

It was a furtive group of people that emerged from the gate that night. There were guards with machine guns lining the walls of Suneel's family house. By a scratching sound above me I knew they were on the flat roof too.

Suneel was especially ill-at-ease. It was as though he couldn't get rid of us quickly enough—scanning the alley and glancing behind him towards the river. He bundled Elly and Andrew into the covered jeep while servants loaded the luggage. Dad helped Mum into the back before climbing in beside the driver. Dad liked being in the front to get the most thrills. Jeep rides in the Himalayan Mountains were not unlike roller-coaster rides.

Then, I don't know how it happened, Mum was moving over for me and in the same moment, Suneel was shouting and pushing me to the ground. The jeep roared off down the lane, splattered with little flashes of light from gunfire that burst out from the dark. I dropped my head down. I couldn't hear the jeep anymore. I prayed they'd get through. Suneel's men were firing towards the river, the shots reverberating so loudly I thought my brain would burst.

Who knows why things happen the way they do. Maybe the driver thought we were all in. Did Suneel push me down because there was no time to lose? Or was it all part of some pre-arranged plan? All I knew was that my family was driving away and I was being shielded from gun fire by Suneel lying practically on top of me.

It was as though I was in a safe, dark pocket in the ground; Suneel was so warm, the gunfire seemed far away. Then I was jolted to reality as I was dragged towards the gate. I got up on my haunches and scuttled in the rest of the way by myself. Suneel was all apologies.

'Your life was more important than your honour,' he was trying to explain, totally embarrassed, as his mother tut-tutted and fussed over me. I was glad. An uneducated man in the street would have left me to die for fear of touching me and ruining my good name.

Suneel rushed off then, after a man threw him an assault rifle. His mother took me into the room where her husband was sitting up in bed, heavily bandaged. I guessed the household had a resident hakim. There was a short exchange between the two, as the khan's face changed from one of welcome to concern. He turned to look at me.

'Beti, I am sorry you are left without your family, but do not worry. They will be safe as you will be. You are as my own daughter until they can return for you. My wife and servants are going to the house of my mother tonight until this trouble is over. You will go with them.'

I almost protested. What if I didn't want to? I could end up in some Himalayan village and never be seen again. But what else was there for me to do? As I nodded my consent I wondered when it would ever be safe to leave with all that noise going on outside.

10

That evening, my heart lifted as we walked up to the Rasheeds' house. There were little dark-headed kids running around in the light from the verandah, the girls in frilly silk dresses unseen in Australian shops, the boys in black pants and embroidered white shirts. Elly had copied me and worn a shalwar qameez. Andrew never joined in on our dressing up. I was beginning to envy him in a way; wherever he went he was still uniquely Andrew.

Even Mum had succumbed to Pakistani national dress, although she had protested while I was getting dressed that Pakistanis who had lived in Australia as long as the Rasheeds wouldn't expect me to wear their clothes. I ignored her, for I knew how much Yasmeen appreciated it when I did.

Yasmeen was already at the door before we'd even pushed the button. One of the little kids had probably spread the word that the Angrez, the English, had arrived. From that moment it felt as if the clock had been turned back three months.

'Jameela!' Yasmeen was so excited she was practically squealing. 'Come in, come in.' Inside, it was more deafening than I expected. It seemed as though everyone was determined to get in as much Pakistani time as they could: the music was louder, the laughs were heartier, the silk clothes were only what I'd seen people wear to weddings in Pakistan, not to a house party. The women were actually dripping with their entire wedding gold. As Yasmeen explained later, it was only times like that when they could wear their best clothes; the women wouldn't wear their gold in public for fear of being misunderstood or having it stolen.

Elly and I were steered to Yasmeen's room. As we passed the lounge, I saw my parents being settled, all the men rising until Mum had sat down. Sitar music was playing as salty snacks bought from the Central Market were being passed around.

Yasmeen's room was unrecognisable. Her bed had been up-ended against the wall and the unmarried female Pakistani population of Adelaide was gyrating to Indian popular songs—the younger the girl, the more modern the dance. Older girls like Yasmeen were dancing the way actresses do in Bollywood movies but girls Elly's age looked just like miniature pop stars in make-up, nail polish and Pakistani high heels made especially for little girls. Elly wasn't even allowed to wear make-up yet, let alone high shoes.

We weren't permitted to stay on the edge, watching. As I was pulled into the centre, I tried to copy Yasmeen. It was like the dancing I'd enjoyed when visiting homes in Pakistan. My friend, Ayesha, had taught Liana and me local dances in boarding school too, usually after lights out.

The recollection made me grin and all of a sudden I was deliriously happy. It wasn't a feeling I expected others to understand. It was like the sun suddenly rose up in my body and shot out of my mouth, bathing me with warm light, and the power of it made me want to dance and laugh. It was like I was Jaime and Jameela, in Australia and Pakistan all at the same time. Before long, the other girls had drawn back and made a circle around Yasmeen and me. They were clapping; Yasmeen was laughing. I was almost crying with excitement when the music suddenly stopped and we both dropped to the floor.

'You dance very well,' Yasmeen gasped out between catching her breath. I knew it was politeness but all the same, I had felt a belonging that must have shown. The song was changed and it was another girl's turn to be clapped into the middle. I was dying for a drink.

As I passed the noise from Shehzad's open door, I wondered how Andrew was getting on. Out of all of us he was the most complacent about returning to Australia. There were more opportunities in Australia, he'd said. I knew Mum and Dad had come back for us but just then I didn't care too much about opportunities. Andrew had never learned to speak Urdu but I needn't have worried—all the Pakistani kids here spoke English. Only a few of the mothers didn't, so I knew Mum would be having fun brushing up her language skills.

Maybe it was still the buoyant feeling from the dancing that made me hum in the kitchen, getting my lemonade, so that I didn't at first notice the guy standing there. He must have been watching me for ages and when he said 'Hello', I dropped the glass I was filling onto the bench.

'Let me help.' He came over and began wiping up the mess before I could pick up the sponge. 'I'm sorry, I did not mean to startle you.'

I was so annoyed. First he'd broken into my warm sunshine feeling and shattered it, and then I couldn't work out why he was talking to me. I mean, why separate the girls from the boys if they're going to make out in the kitchen?

'I hear your name is Jameela?' He was looking straight at me, right into my eyes. Even Shehzad never did that. I tried to look anywhere else except at him. The Australian part of me felt rude, yet I knew it was the right thing to do.

'I'm sorry, I must go,' I managed to mumble.

'Wait a minute.' He put out a hand so that if I didn't stop I'd run right into it. I stood still. 'My name is Shokat.' He was so full of himself and I had thought Shehzad had too much personality. This guy made Shehzad seem like a Himalayan monk. He lounged against the bench as he carried on, 'I am Imran Khan's cousin.'

I'm afraid my mouth fell open in a disgusted sort of amazement. He must have mistaken it for adoration.

'Yes. I am here for the cricket game playing in Adelaide this week. I am the twelfth man.' He made it sound as if he was the captain and I should kiss the end of his bat.

He was grinning like Brer Fox when he caught the rabbit, just picking up the knife and fork. 'I have not been to Adelaide before. Why not you show me the city sights? There must be many places of historical interest.'

Did he think we had an Australian Taj Mahal? How about the Adelaide Fort where thousands died defending South Australian shores from an invading enemy? That was when I pulled my jaw into action and fast.

Without thinking, I gave him the classic Pakistani answer, 'You'll have to ask my father about that. He's right in there.' I waved vaguely in the direction of the lounge. The look on his face was gratifying; the rabbit had got away.

'That's your father? Of course, I—I meant your whole family should come.'

Shehzad sauntered in then. I don't know how much he heard but he took the guy back to his room after giving me a look which was his way of checking I was OK. I could have done with a hug like Danny's right then but I knew Shehzad's upbringing would never allow him to touch me. Yet the new respect and warmth in the way he looked at me made me feel as if he had put his arm around me and made everything right again.

There was a call for the cake-cutting. This was the time when the one-year-old would be in full view and everyone would be allowed to squeeze into the lounge and dining area to witness the cutting of the cake. Elly was right beside me.

'Look at the size of the cake!' Elly could get really impressed with giant food. The cake was a metre-square sponge, filled and topped with confectioner's cream. Elly took a hopeful step forward.

Shehzad was beside me then and managed to apologise for Shokat's behaviour. 'He thought you were the average

Aussie girl, out for a good time. He knows Australian girls date so he thought you would too. But I told him to leave off, you were our family friend.' He laughed. I still couldn't. It had suddenly struck me that my strategy with Shokat would never work with an average Australian guy. What if one propositioned me? I couldn't very well say, 'Go ask my father.' The guy would curl up laughing.

'Is he really Imran Khan's cousin?'

'Probably—six times removed through marriage. He's no doubt found it works with Australian girls.'

'I'm not a regular Australian girl.'

Shehzad stopped grinning. 'No, you're not. And Shokat wants a formal introduction now. He's so impressed that you understand Pakistani customs.'

I was about to say 'don't bother', when Shehzad continued. 'But don't worry. He probably just wants an Australian visa and the request wouldn't get past my father anyway—he's the chairperson of the Pak-Australian Association.'

'Thanks.' I couldn't help thinking how standing there beside him made me feel as if I were with Andrew. For all his quietness, Andrew could make you feel that deep down the things that truly matter don't change.

'Shehzad, what year are you in?'

'Eleven.'

'Do you find it hard?'

'Not bad. Fortunately, we came when I was young enough, so I don't have trouble with English. Dad always spoke it to me anyway. He said that was the sure way not to have problems later. They put me back a year too, so I find it easier than most of my cousins.'

'Will you stay?'

'Sure. My parents have a good attitude about Australia. And besides, I want to be a doctor and I don't want to go through all the trouble Dad did upgrading his qualifications for the medical board here. He was a top specialist in Lahore. Here, he's a doctor like the rest of them in the hospital. But at least he's practising, I guess.'

'It's hard gaining a high enough score to get into medicine.'

'I know but I'll study like crazy. Most kids here don't work hard. They don't know what it's like to want something because your whole family depends on it.'

I was lost in thought. Andrew worked hard but most of the kids in my class didn't. Kate and Debra talked their way through every lesson. I had no idea how they ever found time to finish their assignments.

Everyone clapped as the cake was cut. The little cousin was plump, smiling and looked like a sugar plum fairy, swathed in chiffon, frills and lace, with bows in her hair. She was being passed around the aunties and uncles to have her photo taken. First birthdays were a big deal in Pakistan. A lady told me once it came from the time, not so long ago, when staying alive for the first year was so risky that if babies reached a year, they had a good chance of reaching adulthood.

The baby had just been passed to a girl my age. She stood out with her short, stylish hair, jeans and long shirt.

She reminded me of someone and when she laughed to her neighbour over the head of the baby, I remembered. The movies. She was the girl at the movies I thought looked like a Pakistani.

'Shehzad, who's that girl over there?'

He turned to see where I was looking. He didn't hesitate like Yasmeen might have. 'That's Rosina, my twin sister. Come, I'll introduce you. You should get on well together.'

With mixed feelings I followed him, squeezing past ladies' knees and trying not to brush against any guys. Did she see me that day? Then she would have seen Danny. But she was with a boy too. We were in the same boat, weren't we? Then I remembered Danny's comments about Greek girls and I decided to hold my tongue. Maybe no one knew where she was that day.

Shehzad introduced me as Jaime, not Jameela.

'Hi!' She had such expressive brown eyes, the first thing I noticed. Her accent was like Shehzad's and she always seemed to be laughing. Yet I knew she wasn't happy. I think it was her eyes—her laugh never seemed to reach them.

We sat together, eating the cake that was being passed around with forks, plates and napkins that said 'Happy Birthday, Fozia' on them. I never mentioned the movies, nor did she. But she told me heaps of stories about school and her friends. When she asked me about school, I couldn't say much really. It wasn't my whole life as it seemed to be for her, nor could I talk about Danny. I could tell she wouldn't want to hear about my favourite topic (Pakistan) so I kept asking general questions to keep her talking.

'Have you ever been back to Pakistan?' I didn't mean to ask that but all nerve endings in my brain led to Pakistan sooner or later.

'Sure. But I'll never go again.'

'Why?' I wasn't ready for her reaction. It was almost physical in its intensity, even though she laughed at the end.

'It was a dirty, smelly place. Beggars everywhere, clawing at you. No social help, no one cared. They actually eat goats' heads and they don't have proper stoves in their houses. Nah, not for me.'

The words weren't connected but I got her meaning loud and clear. At times I couldn't put Australia in a logical sentence either. I found it unbelievable that this was Yasmeen's sister—that two people could look at the same thing yet describe something totally different.

Just then the birthday girl was dropped in my lap so we could pose for a photo. She did the rounds until she was screaming with fatigue and Shehzad picked her up as gently as Danny had ever held me and carried her off to a quieter part of the house.

Yasmeen found me then to tell me of the dancing coming up next. With the baby gone everyone looked as if they were settling down for a long night. Hand drums called tablas were brought in and a man had a sitar. A young man began dancing.

Most of the girls had gone back to Yasmeen's room, but Elly's eyes were beginning to glaze over and Mum had her weary 'quick get me home I'm turning into a pumpkin' look. Dad was like an old clock that had been wound up for the first time in years. It was so good to see that, but Mum was making faces at him from across the room. I knew what that meant.

I glanced at the man dancing. Yasmeen had her back to him and no wonder. It was so hard to rip my eyes away; his dance looked like a cross between some tribal dance and Michael Jackson's moonwalk. It was hard to believe how so-called moral people could dance like that. All the older women were clapping and laughing. Yasmeen was murmuring that the real dancing was going to be in her room as she tried to pull me away.

Unfortunately, at that point, my father stood up. Mum's facial gymnastics had finally worked. Dad managed to pick his way across the room amid the dancing to lift up Elly and we all said 'goodbye' at the door amid many 'so soon?'s.

Mum went on in the car about the 'nice girl in jeans', most probably pressing home her earlier point about my clothes. But she didn't know what Rosina may have gone through to wear those jeans. Maybe I would never know it all, either. Did we always have to fall from grace in one group to be accepted in another?

That night I dreamed of Suneel. He was handing me into the jeep. The fighting had stopped for a while. It was the middle of the night. I had no luggage; mine had gone with my family.

Suneel offered me a package …

'Open this when you get to my grandmother's. It will make me happy to see you wear it.'

His mother was smiling as if it had been her idea. Then his words struck home, making me feel as if I'd found gold. He was going to see me wear it? He would come? Later? The hope must have shown in my eyes, for he touched me. Actually touched me, not by accident, not shielding me; he consciously touched the side of my face, caressing it as though it was important enough to memorise. I almost thought he would kiss me. Would he have? If his mother wasn't there?

'Keep safe, little one. Until we meet again.' His eyes looked right into mine as the jeep's engine revved up. It was so unusual, so uncultural for him to do that; it was like a declaration, yet his mother kept smiling.

11

It was a wonder I could keep my eyes open the next day at school. In Pakistan too, families would have parties on the very day of the birthday whether people had to go to work next day or not. Everything stopped for celebrations. A whole week's holiday could be taken for attending a family wedding.

I'd woken that morning with thoughts of Suneel. Dreams do that to me. Even if I don't like a person much but dream about them being nice, I see them in an entirely different light the next day. Suneel was the only thing I could concentrate on. At least he was one of my assignments.

> The jeep had finally come to a stop. I was glad, as I felt queasy from the lurching of the vehicle on the winding road and through narrow, mountain passes. Many times I'd heard water rushing close by; at other times, it'd seemed hundreds of feet below us. Now it was almost dawn. I could still hear running water as we left the jeep—with me clutching Suneel's package—and made our way towards the square, wooden structures that I knew would make up Suneel's grandmother's village.

'This is Suneel's village,' his mother said.

'Suneel's?'

'Ji, not only did he grow up here, but even while his father still lives, he is the head of it, so to speak. One day he will rule this whole valley of Rumbur.'

'How will he do that?'

'Times are changing. It used to be birth alone that gave our family that right. Now there are elections. In the first election a few years ago, we were voted in to keep doing the work we have always done for our people. Who knows? Maybe this election will be the same. I hope so, for Suneel and his father understand these people. They are our people.'

I hoped so too, if that was what Suneel wanted.

We didn't make it halfway to the houses set into the hillside before swarms of youngsters came hurtling down the slopes to welcome us with giggles, shy smiles and touches on our arms and hands. Suneel's mother knew most of them by name and hugged them indiscriminately as we made our way slowly up the hill.

By the time we reached a house that looked like all the others with its wooden and unbaked mud brick layers, there were men and young girls smiling a welcome as we were guided onto a plank bridge that led to a verandah. I ducked my head as a giggling girl of my own age, in a long black dress embroidered with yellow and red thread, lifted the curtain over the door for me to enter.

Inside, preparations for breakfast had begun. There was a tandoori-like oven set into the middle of the floor and two older girls, also in black dresses, were making their own style of flat bread. There were no windows and the smoke from the fire made it difficult to see at first until I became used to the darkened room. I was led to an old woman sitting cross-legged on a stringed bed.

She spoke, but I didn't understand. I turned to Suneel's mother for help and she nodded me forward.

'This is Suneel's grandmother. She says "welcome". A wedding is always a happy time and Suneel's will be the best of all.'

So soon? I wondered which one of the girls I'd seen was chosen for him and I realised with a dead feeling in my stomach that I didn't want any of them to have him. I was so involved in my own jealous thoughts that I missed the next thing his mother said. She patted my package with a smile and I was being led to sit by the fire.

One of the girls spoke to me, her shy smile making her eyes crinkle. They were green, like Suneel's.

His mother translated, 'She said that it is very exciting having you come. She hasn't met an Australian person before.' I smiled my thanks and had a better look at all the girls. They all had skin as fair as Suneel's; their eyes were his colour. Their hair, braided at the front where I'd wear a fringe, and the tiny plaits down each side were dark brown like his, not black.

Just then a younger girl sat behind me and started plaiting my hair into five braids, like theirs, putting coloured clips in the side and a cowrie-shell headdress on the top. Another girl came towards me, giggling, as she carried a black dress with the red and yellow embroidery around the neck and hem. They pulled off my Pakistani shirt and lowered the black dress over my head, tying a cloth belt around my waist while at the same time bunching the front up over the belt. Then hundreds of tiny red and white beads threaded together were tied round my neck.

Suneel's mother had also changed.

'They're very kind,' I whispered to her. 'But what is going on? Why did you change? Why do they all wear black?'

'My dear, we are the Kalasha. We women always have worn black ever since anyone can remember, since Sekandar.' Sekandar, Alexander... so that's where they got those green eyes and brown hair.

'And you, my dear,' she held me at arm's length and looked me up and down, 'you look the perfect Kalasha princess.'

'I—'

'Jaime.'

Oh, no. Mr Bolden. I jumped guiltily. At least I was in the right class this time.

'Could you see me please and bring your English folder?'

I sighed. He already had the rough draft of my assignment on Suneel laid out on his desk. Super organised was Mr Bolden. Some of the other kids were talking quietly. Correction: all of the other kids were talking quietly, except Billy. He was always loud. It was something I still found hard to get used to: that constant talking in class even when the teacher was giving instructions.

Mr Bolden cleared his throat as I sat down. 'I'd like to ask you some questions, if you don't mind, Jaime.' It was his eyebrows rather than his tone of voice which made it into a request, so I nodded. Growing up in another culture made me more aware of body language. In Pakistan it was often the only clue I had to what was going on.

'First of all, you have good style. I feel you on the paper, in the words; I get a clear picture as I read.' I pursed my lips. That was the sugar on the pill. Now for the rest.

'But why did you stop writing your personal journal, the one you were writing to Pakistan? I think you would have found it beneficial to continue it.'

How could I explain? In one way I'd been so caught up with Suneel's story that I'd forgotten I hadn't kept on with the journal. In another way Suneel's story was my journal, what I thought about Pakistan, but it was hard to explain.

'Um, I think I didn't do it anymore because the things that were happening to me were too foreign for Pakistan to understand. I mean, none of it added up. After a while, I didn't notice shorts on men and I started being friends with a guy. In Pakistan that's immoral, but it's not here. I suppose I could have written in the journal about Yasmeen, but once I'd met her I didn't need to anymore.'

'So you wrote the story about Suneel.'

I nodded. 'Even Yasmeen wouldn't understand everything I'm going through, not the Australian stuff. Suneel seems the only safe topic of thought at times. It all happens the way I want it to. It's Pakistan but I'm still me.'

I drew in a deep breath. I didn't know where all that came from. I hadn't actually thought it all out like that before. Mr Bolden was chewing his bottom lip as he watched me. Billy was growing louder and I was sure he was throwing paper across the room, but Mr Bolden didn't seem to notice.

'I think you're too hard on yourself, Jaime. You are doing well for the length of time you've been here. You've settled in, made friends…'

Yeah, Danny and Yasmeen. You couldn't call Kate a friend. I hadn't made it with the girls at all, really.

'It takes time to settle and you will.' Easy for him to say. He didn't know the stuff some of the kids threw at me or what I thought about. I couldn't stand the way adults would look at the outside and if everything looked in working order, they'd think everything was fine, yet they couldn't see the rust eating away underneath.

'The story about Suneel—' he sounded as if he was trying not to step on a mine '— did it really happen?'

Did it really happen? Of course. It's happening now, isn't it?

'No, not all of it. We were on holiday up in the mountains in Chitral just before election time. We didn't realise it would blow up like that. The riot, everything about that is true. The bazaar was shot up, people were killed. It happens here too, in shopping malls and for no reason.'

Why did I suddenly feel as if I had to justify it? He hadn't looked disapproving. I went back to the story.

'Suneel's family got us a flight out of the valley the next day. My family left together. I hardly spoke to Suneel actually. The social customs there are very strict.'

Mr Bolden nodded. By the way he kept fiddling with his pen and glancing at me, I knew he had more to say. 'I would like to keep seeing the story for as long as you write it, if you don't mind. You've almost got enough material to satisfy the assignment requirements but I'd be interested in hearing what happens.'

I was surprised. There I was, steeling myself for the disapproval that was sure to come. I mean, who in their right mind creates stories to make themselves feel better? Already I was feeling a little guilty about it as it was starting to grip me like a compulsion, and I felt too embarrassed to tell anyone. Mr Bolden was the only one who knew. In the beginning, I'd forgotten about him being real flesh and blood, reading *me*, sharing a secret part of my life. Of course in the beginning I didn't expect it to become so personal.

At first, I thought he was trying reverse psychology. Like, tell a kid to stay up to midnight and he'll go to bed at ten. Mum had tried it on Andrew but it didn't take long before he woke up to it. Did Mr Bolden really mean it was a good idea to write the story? Maybe he knew, before I did, just how much the story was a way I could sort out my feelings in an environment where I didn't have to worry about new language cues and conflicting ways of doing things.

I wondered how much of my feelings actually showed on my face, for Mr Bolden suddenly leaned a little closer over the desk. 'Jaime, we don't have to be frightened of the past. Let your memory have its way, remember the good. God can turn the "might have been" into a positive way of life.' He chewed his lip as if he wasn't sure what I'd do with his advice.

I was unusually speechless. It was the realisation that he had made such an effort to understand me. He knew I was scared.

'I think we have quite a bit in common,' he went on.

I pricked up my ears; this'd be good. 'When I was younger than you I came out with my family from England.'

'Really, sir? I wouldn't have known.'

He grinned ruefully. 'I lost my accent quickly due to numerous playground beatings. It was tougher in those days.'

It was?

'But Jaime, every non-indigenous person here came from somewhere else. Take me. I was brought up to be thankful I was here but I still like tea better than beer. There are some things I don't care for but I get on with life. There are things I don't like about England too.'

I knew then he was wrong: we didn't have much in common, because there was nothing I didn't like about Pakistan.

That afternoon as I stepped off the bus I couldn't help remembering what Mr Bolden said. He'd finished with the classic 'come and talk to me anytime'. I'd thanked him with a show of understanding and stability and said it wouldn't be necessary. Whether or not I had convinced him, I still wasn't sure he wouldn't go blabbing off to the other staff members about 'Jaime Richards who writes weird stories'.

I mightn't have admitted it then but until that talk with him I'd felt kind of childish for starting a story off true, then changing it to the way I'd wanted. Now I felt relaxed about it. It wasn't a dumb thing to do after all.

Elly was pleased I was in a good mood. Her eyes shone hope like they do when she thinks I'm going to spend time with her. How could I tell her I had heaps of homework?

I wasn't the only one in a good mood that night. Dad had finally found a job. No more standing in lines at the social security office for him. To celebrate he bought a pizza, one of the double deals— Coke, garlic bread, the lot.

'So, what's the job, Dad?' I was on my second piece of pizza. Elly and Andrew had most probably lost count. In all fairness, they were still growing. Since I wasn't sure if I'd stopped or not, I didn't take too many chances when it came to pizza and Coke.

Dad was all smiles. He was starting to get his bounce back. 'It's with the Department of Immigration. They have a refugee association and need aid workers to help refugees settle in the area. I'll be working with the Afghan sector. There are more coming into the northern suburbs now and they need a lot of TLC after what they've been through in Afghanistan. Especially the ones who have been in detention.'

It sounded exciting work and poor me had to go to

school every day. 'I wish I could come with you.'

'Perhaps you could. We can visit families on weekends. Everyone will need help with their English and there are sure to be kids.'

'You were an aid worker in Pakistan too, Daddy,' piped up Elly.

'Yep, they call it "social worker" here.' I knew Dad would be in his element. He'd had a way with languages; he was fluent in Urdu and Dari and understood bits of others as well. As Mum pointed out, it would have been his languages that got him the job, as the social workers were usually chosen from their own cultural group.

There was a lot to think about that night. Just before I'd left Mr Bolden, he'd said that I could see a little further than the average sixteen-year-old, that it was my differences that made me 'me', and maybe I should be accepting of them rather than worrying about them too much. But I wondered, lying there somewhere between waking and dreaming, how did one do that?

12

Would you believe it? I now had a new friend at school. I had taken Blake's advice and tried to think of someone to take me to town. Mum used to say first impressions were often the right ones so I picked Sara, fully expecting her to say 'no' after the nose pin episode. She accepted. I don't know who was the more surprised about the whole thing—her or me.

Sara didn't talk as much as me so it left me plenty of scope for being myself. I could never get a word in sideways with Kate and Debra, not that their conversations were remotely uplifting. Actually, they were a lot like eating a pomegranate: once you'd peeled away all the four letter words and slang, it only left the seeds, not much for the digestive juices to get excited about.

'Why did you ask me to take you to town?' Sara asked on the train, emphasis on the 'me'. I'd already gritted my teeth and outlined the 'I need you' bit.

'I wanted to get to know you better. I did on the first day too, honest. I'm so sorry I upset you with the nose pin story. I shouldn't have kept on and on. It was a bad day all round.'

'Was it really like that?'

'The pin?'

She nodded.

'Sure it was. Worse, really. Then there was the ten days after when the silver wire had to be changed for the stud.' I checked her face; her colour was still good, so I continued. 'The only other trouble we had was when Dad bought me the tiny diamond and neither Mum nor I could get it in. We did in the end, though, and I vowed never to take it out again.' I went quiet after that. There were times it still hurt that I couldn't wear it anymore.

'I am sorry, you know.' Sara was looking so sympathetic that I knew I had another friend. Where was she four months ago? I grinned. 'Was I such a pain at the beginning of the year?'

The slight movement of her head was almost a nod, like a sneeze that got stifled. Then she said, 'I thought I'd like you since you were so different from Kate and that mob, but I didn't know what to say to you. Especially after the pin. I've never been anywhere. It takes a big effort for me to even remember there's a world out there at all. I knew I'd sound dumb and you knew so much.'

Without meaning to, she made it sound as if I'd been so full of myself. I tried to think back. How many times had I said 'when I was in Pakistan' with a superior air just because I was trying to make myself feel better? Some of the boys still ribbed me on that one in a singsong voice. Then there were the times (and still were) when I knew a better way to do something. Did it show? What about the times in conversations when I'd attacked the media or told someone off for being racist?

'I'm sorry.'

'What for?'

'For being difficult to get along with. I wouldn't have liked it if someone came over to Pakistan while we were there and told us we were doing everything wrong. I think I was just trying to see where I fitted in. I still am.'

'I don't think you're difficult, especially not now I know you. Just ask me anything and I'll help in any way I can.'

Now Sara was my constant companion. She told me things and stopped me before I stumbled into gaping holes. Like the time Debra made a snide comment about a couple of guys holding hands at the bus stop. I was still stupid enough at that point to ask what she meant. All I got were ill-disguised giggles and snorts and 'where have you been, Jaime Richards?'

Sara leaned closer. 'Leave it. They're gay.'

I was rocked into silence and checked the guys out from under my eyelashes. Really, I would never have noticed. All the guys in Pakistan walked around like that, holding hands, arms around each other and they weren't necessarily gay. It was just their custom. In a place where fraternising between opposite sexes was forbidden in public, affection was sure to appear elsewhere.

I sneaked a look at Kate. She and Debra were pink with withheld mirth and scorn. Sara's face was like a blank sheet. I couldn't help thinking that the tolerant laws of this country were at odds with the way people really thought.

Just as Kate had pointed out to me months ago about Danny and discrimination, most issues at street level were like a steaming compost heap, yet no one seemed to notice the heat.

I asked Dad about it that night. He said it was like that in Pakistan too, especially during the time after September 11 and the recent bomb attacks. 'Each time the government made a decision and publicised their alliance with the West. Yet what happened at street level, Jaime?' I remembered the tension, the riots, the processions of the men in the bazaars, the deep regret that it had ever happened.

'Well, during the drone and missile attacks, the people sided with the Taliban.'

'Yes, though not all, Jaime. Most of the non-extremists realised the government's way was best at the time, even though it meant siding with the West.'

I nodded, deep in thought. Dad made it seem normal. All the same, I didn't like Pakistan put on the same level as something happening here. There wasn't any comparison, was there?

I went to prise Andrew off the computer to type up more of my story about Suneel. It was getting harder to find time for it. We only had one computer and I didn't have an iPad yet like other kids at school.

Fortunately, he was in the kitchen making supplementary food: four pieces of toast and Vegemite. I hated Vegemite.

The first day in the tiny village was passing well. I was taking more of the rice and meat sauce with the flat bread and eating it with my fingers. There was a huge plate of walnuts and oranges on the floor in front of us. I'd found someone else who spoke some English. Her name was Rushda.

'You do like here?' she asked.

My mouth was full so I inclined my head and she continued. 'We wish to build school in this valley. Children are mistreated in government school.'

I wondered why but I still had a mouthful and couldn't ask.

'You can teach English?' she asked when I finished chewing.

'Ji.' I grinned. It was embarrassing trying to hold a conversation and eating at the same time. I hadn't thought about teaching, with two years of high school still to go, but teaching English to people who didn't know any at all sounded fun.

I wondered what she was on about. 'Do you want help with your homework?'

'Nay, I finish school. We marry at fifteen. I think I fifteen.' She giggled. I thought it interesting she didn't know how old she was. She certainly looked fifteen or older. 'Our boys go in university. Suneel went to Islamabad for study.' So that was how he had that worldly air and perfect English with an accent that sounded like Imran Khan's when he was interviewed on TV.

Rushda peeled an orange for me. Then she cracked nuts and handed me some. I protested. I knew I was the guest, but they didn't have to do everything for me.

'It okay. I do for you. I your friend. I help you. For always.'

The 'always' got to me. She made it sound as though we wouldn't just be writing letters over the years. How could she be always with me?

'Come.' She stood up then. 'We go to river.'

I followed her out, wondering who would wash the cooking pots. Outside, the sun was dazzling after the dark of the windowless room. She guided me down the wooden plank and we made our way through the trees towards the river.

'This is a beautiful place, Rushda.'

'Ji,' was all she said, but she looked pleased.

She must have been a clever girl in school to learn English as well as she had. I wondered if she was the one they'd chosen for Suneel.

'Here,' she said, as we reached the rocks by the river. 'We sit here, we watch.' Not far away many other girls our age were washing clothes, banging stubborn stains on the rocks to cleanse them, then washing and rinsing in the running water.

'Do you drink from this water?' I asked, watching one girl with her sandals off, dragging in a contrary goat.

Rushda waved upstream. 'From there. Suneel say not here. He learn much in city. He very intelligent, young but good man.' She sounded as if she wanted to convince me but she needn't have made the effort. I'd already noticed.

Watching the goat reminded me of the first time I saw him. 'Rushda, does Suneel like goats? Does he look after them?'

The look she cast me could have scorched a bush in winter. 'Never. Suneel, son of khan.'

'I saw him in a goat field one day.'

'Maybe he tell goat boy work to do. Goat boys very stupid.'

I grinned. 'Shall we help wash the clothes?' I stood but she pulled me down so quickly I winced.

'Nay.' She looked unusually tense. 'We sit here. You enjoy. You not happy?'

As I nodded, she relaxed. She took a wooden comb from under a rock then and started undoing some of my plaits and combing them gently so that I almost fell asleep.

13

It was Friday night. Danny and his family were finally coming over for dinner. Mum was one of those mothers who invited your friends over (especially boys) in the effort to bring everything into the light of day so nothing can lurk behind the skirting boards. Though in my case there was nothing to lurk. Danny was just my friend.

Mum was in a bit of a whirl worrying whether Greek people would like what she'd cooked. I'd given up explaining how Danny was Australian; she still referred to him as 'Jaime's nice Greek friend from school.' After I'd helped as much as I could there was plenty of time to spare, so I crept into Andrew's room to type up more of Suneel's story.

> Little things were starting to concern me. I'd been a guest in a village before and knew good treatment was given to guests, but I was sure there were things said and done that weren't necessary.
>
> Take the charpai beds for instance. There were only two in the whole house. The grandmother had one and I presumed the mother of the girls in the house would have the other. They brought in one for Suneel's mother but they motioned me onto the one

beside his grandmother. The lady of the house was smiling but I felt uncomfortable climbing into a bed when I knew a woman thirty years my senior would sleep on the floor.

When I remonstrated with Suneel's mother, she just waved her hand as she made the cryptic statement: 'It is expected. Do not argue.'

All the girls slept in the room. The men settled out on the verandah. I watched the girls' headdresses and sandals come off, but each one lay down in their dresses and beads.

'Rushda, why do some girls have headdresses like mine and yours, and some have larger ones with more shells?'

'They are for married girls.'

I stared at one headdress as a young married girl took it off and hung it on the wall. It had an elaborate V-shaped shell design and a red pompom tuft on top.

Rushda settled herself on a mat as close to my bed as she could manage. If I had to get out of bed in the middle of the night, I couldn't hope to miss stepping on her. As I put my head on the pillow, I had the disconcerting thought that this was probably the very reason she was there.

I leaned over the edge. 'Rushda,' I whispered.

'Ji, bibi.' The term of respect unnerved me so that at first I couldn't go on. I'd only ever heard it used to address people much older than oneself or of higher rank. 'Rushda?'

'Ji?' she replied again and I suddenly realised the eternal patience in her tone was that of a servant, one chosen to serve, and one proud to be chosen.

An idea came to my mind—I was surprised that I hadn't thought of it before—an idea that at once frightened me yet filled me with intense excitement and joy.

'Rushda, why am I here?'

'Do you not know?'

'No.' I held my breath. Maybe I did know.

'Have you not looked in your gift from Suneel?'

It was under my pillow. I knew it was a shell headdress but I hadn't taken it out since the girls had given me one already and I didn't want to offend. I took it out now. It was different from my other one; I hadn't realised. It had a triangular shape, the woollen tuft on top, many more shells, many more than I had even seen on the married girls' headdresses that they wore when they went out. There were beads and coloured stones set into the top and front piece. It was the headdress of a princess.

'Why me? I'm not Kalasha. Why me?'

'It is Suneel's wish.'

'He doesn't know me.'

'It is not custom to know bride. Besides, it is his wish. The mother of Suneel was like you.'

Suneel's mother? I looked over at the older woman on the bed beside me. She was nothing like me.

What could Rushda mean?

'Jaime! Quick!' Mum was in panic mode. I only had time to hit the save key. When Mum yelled like that it usually meant the roasting pan was falling out of one hand while she was trying to stir the gravy with the other. I rushed out to the kitchen, meaning to do more of Suneel's story later.

Later never came, for as soon as I rescued the roasting pan, the doorbell rang and the house was immediately full of happy, laughing people. Only Danny, his mum and dad, and two of his little sisters came, but his parents were as large as life, just as Dad was beginning to be again, so that our house seemed much smaller than it was.

In no time we were all squashed around our oval table and Mum's roast was disappearing off the serving plates at a speed equal to Elly's and Andrew's usual track record.

Dad and Mr Dimitriadis were in the middle of one of those jokes where you can't remember who started it, when I felt a feather-touch on my foot. I looked up, fully expecting Elly to be grinning, pretending she hadn't done it when Danny winked at me. I quickly shovelled peas onto my fork, but not before I noticed Elly's gaping mouth as she stared at Danny. She had hardly touched her dinner. I suppose Danny would look to Elly like a hero out of one of her books—what she'd call 'drop dead gorgeous'. I sneaked another look at him myself. I guess there was good reason to have a second look, especially with him grinning at me like that. I winked back. Maybe it wouldn't be a bad idea to be going out with Danny.

The evening raced on: dessert, coffee, Greek biscuits that Mrs Dimitriadis had brought, more coffee. Andrew got tired of it after a while and invited Danny into his room to see his latest computer game. Elly had long since taken the little girls into her room to see the baby mice. Danny waved as he followed Andrew. We'd had just as much fun from opposite sides of the room, saying nothing, as we'd ever had together at school talking through lunch.

It wasn't until I saw Andrew come out into the kitchen for drinks that I remembered I'd left my story on the screen. I hadn't had time to go back and exit. Suddenly I felt as though I'd left my diary open on the billboard at the bus stop in giant print. What if Andrew had read it? I excused myself from the conversation with Mrs Dimitriadis and practically ran to Andrew's room.

Danny was sitting at the computer. It looked as if he were playing a game, his fingers hovering over the scrolling keys, his head bent forward in interest. I heaved a sigh of relief. But it was short-lived. He swung around on the swivel chair to face me; behind him I could see the screen. Suneel's name jumped out at me, naked and accusing for leaving him there. Danny had actually scrolled back right through my story, my private work, my life. I rushed forward and closed the document.

'How dare you! Read my stuff like that!'

'You left it there.'

'It was an accident. You should have seen straight away it was private.'

'I'm glad I saw it.' He stood up then; his eyes were darker than usual and had lost their shine. 'I knew there had to be another guy, maybe not here, over there, but this,' he glanced at the screen, 'it's too hard playing second fiddle to a country, some dream, a guy who's not even real. He's not, is he?'

I didn't hear the hope or desperation then, I was too angry. 'Yes, he is. Well, sort of.' I don't think Danny was listening.

'If it was another guy here, I'd know what to do, but this is no challenge. There's nothing left to fight with. I can't compete with your mind—some myth of your imagination.'

'What are you talking about? What's it got to do with you anyway? This is my English assignment. It's an allegory, some way to write how I feel.'

'Jaime, you don't need this crap. Have you ever met this guy?' He didn't wait for me to answer. 'Even if you had he'd be married off to a Himalayan princess by now.' Danny moved closer. He had a look on his face like I once saw on a Pakistani's when he was about to beat his wife for talking to a guy.

Did I actually shrink against the wall? I can't remember. Then his whole attitude suddenly changed. Talk about Continental volatility.

His voice was softer. 'Jaime, you're holding onto too much. Don't you see? You're not letting yourself see what's here. Sure, there's a lot of bad stuff, but there's good too. Don't throw away today. Let yourself feel for where you are now.'

I wondered what might have happened next if Andrew hadn't come in then with two mugs of coffee. Would things have turned out differently? But I didn't hang around. My anger had changed into something that was threatening to spill down the front of me and I didn't want anyone to see.

Let Mum think up some excuse why I went to bed early without saying goodnight.

Later, as I cooled down and stopped crying, I felt sorry for Danny. It would be devastating to find a story written by a girl you cared for and discover you weren't in it yourself. I guessed that was where 'the rubber hit the road', as Dad used to say. Danny must have been hanging out for me to be ready to be more than a friend. Otherwise would a platonic friend get so upset over something like that?

And that bit about 'feeling' for here. Was I dead? I didn't stop myself seeing and feeling things, did I? Maybe I had been too critical about the Australian way of doing things. But how do you stop thinking things that you know are true?

Yet however much I tried to give Danny the benefit of the doubt, it still stung that he'd called my story crap. That bit I took very personally.

14

Fortunately I didn't run into Danny on Monday. I wouldn't have known how to handle it. Sara knew there was something wrong. I would usually tell her everything, though not about Suneel, of course. So I told her I'd had a fight with Danny. She was big on forgiveness and having a talk with him. She liked Danny, although she confided she wouldn't be allowed to go out with him. I just stared at her when she told me that, like 'now you tell me'.

I wanted to be friends with Danny again, but it still didn't take away that 'totally misunderstood' feeling. It hurt because I thought he had understood. I guess it's when expectations are too high that we get the most disappointed. Maybe that goes for countries as well as for guys. Maybe Danny too; perhaps he'd expected too much from me, wanted what I couldn't give. Even though I didn't believe everything Kate said, I was beginning to realise that being a girlfriend to Danny would involve more than a few kisses in his car at night.

I was toying with the idea of having a talk with Mr Bolden and taking a later bus home when Elly raced up breathless to ride home with me. The talk would keep, Elly couldn't, so amid her chattering we headed for the bus. It's funny how things work out, for in making that one simple decision, I changed so much, even though I didn't sense it until ages after.

Elly saw the police car first. I usually looked the other way when I saw police. I guess that came from living in Pakistan. When we were stopped for a breathalyser test when we'd only been in Australia a month, I was certain the test would turn up positive even though Dad hardly ever drank. I'd learnt police couldn't always be trusted.

'Hey, Jaime. They've got a little kid.' In Elly's megaphone whisper it sounded as though the police had abducted the poor little guy. I risked a look. The kid was crying and shaking his head every time the policeman tried to lift him up, obviously to put him in the car, and the kid didn't want to cooperate.

It was Elly who saved the day. 'Doesn't he look like someone we know from Pakistan?' I took a good look. He wasn't, but she wasn't far off the mark. He was an Afghan. I could tell; you get used to picking which areas people come from when you've lived in a place like Pakistan. He had the fairer features and dark curly hair that we saw so often on the Afghan refugees that poured into Islamabad, seeking political asylum.

I hardly missed a heartbeat; Dad would be so proud of me. Approaching the policeman, I said, 'Excuse me, but I might be able to help.'

He may never know what courage it took for me to talk to him. I'd never spoken to a policeman before. He looked annoyed at first, like 'get lost kid can't you see I'm busy' but the little guy suddenly stopped crying. He was looking at me as if I were the Queen of Sheba. Maybe it was the plaits I was wearing that day; Afghan girls wore them too, or maybe he'd been told a fairy with a white face would grant him a wish one day (they do get told the most interesting fibs to keep them quiet). Whatever it was, it sure worked. I didn't know any Dari or Pushtu though, like Dad, so I tried Urdu.

'What is your name?' I asked, sitting on my haunches.

It took him a while to answer as if he wasn't expecting me to be able to say anything he understood.

'Ali.'

'Where do you live, Ali?'

He only looked about four and he spoke the Urdu lispingly, making it hard to understand. When he answered, I thought he said 'Peshawar'. He sure was a long way from home. Five months ago I would have said, 'Hey, tell me about it.'

'Did you live in Peshawar, Ali?'

He nodded. He was better at understanding than speaking.

'Do you live in Australia now?'

He nodded again. 'Is your family here?'

His eyes filled with tears as he nodded again.

'Do you live here in Salisbury?' Blank. 'Salisbury' wasn't part of his vocabulary yet. I turned to the policeman.

'He's an Afghan refugee. They must have only just moved into the area.' I could tell the police officer was impressed. 'I think if you take him to the Migrant Resource Centre, they'll know where he lives. My father works there.'

Men can be so helpless sometimes. 'But I can't get him into the car.'

I suddenly saw the policeman as an ordinary guy. I grinned and turned around to Ali. I held out my arms and he walked straight in as I picked him up.

'Ali, this policeman will take you home.' The little kid stiffened as he pulled away and I knew what was wrong. I set him down again.

'Ali, in Australia the policemen are good men. Not like Pakistan.' What was I saying? I felt like a traitor, but it was true. Some of the police in Pakistan were merciless to the Afghans and to others as well, asking for bribes to supplement their meagre income and often framing innocent people for the same reason.

'This man will not beat you, nor will he ask your father for money. It is different here. You are in Australia now.'

The boy smiled tentatively and I hugged him close as I swallowed down a lump in my throat. Here he was, still afraid of the very things that his parents would have brought him here to save him from: police corruption, war, political unrest and the threat of prison or death.

'You are safe in Australia, Ali.' I hoped I was telling the truth.

The boy smiled widely and nodded as though he'd been told that before and I'd just confirmed it.

The poor policeman hadn't understood a word, only that I'd managed to bring a terrified boy to the brink of smiling at him. 'What was wrong?'

I shrugged, a little embarrassed. 'The police in Pakistan sometimes ill-treat the refugees. He was frightened of you, your uniform, the car, everything. They're often told the police will carry them away if they're naughty or go too close. At times it's a good-behaviour trick, but sometimes it's true. Either that or he's been in a detention centre and thinks you're one of the guards.'

The policeman shook his head in frustration. 'But how can people live like that? Under so much fear? Here kids are taught from kindergarten to get on with the police. They come to the station. Hear the siren. I even go to schools to tell them stories about what we do.'

It was my turn to be surprised. 'You do?'

'How else do you get the respect necessary for law and order?'

How indeed. He didn't know the rigid set of rules that everyone knew about in Pakistan, where in some areas a man could still get his hand cut off for stealing and a woman stoned for adultery. Dad had come in one day, shaking, from the bazaar. He'd just seen a man publicly whipped for rape. There were no more rapes in the village that year. I didn't think the policeman would understand all that so I picked up Ali again.

'Would you mind coming too, miss? You're doing such a good job.'

Elly was impressed; I could tell by the way she pushed me towards the car before I could even think.

'Do you think he'll put the siren on?' Elly's whispers

always sounded staged and I saw the police officer smile.

'They only do that for emergencies,' I whispered back. Ali tightened his grasp around my neck as he stared out of the window. I wondered what was going on in his little head. I was around his age when I first went to Pakistan. I can't remember much but Mum said I became very shy (a source of concern apparently) and had nightmares. After six months I was fine, playing with the kids next door, totally accepting of my environment. I hugged Ali tighter.

I wanted him to have a good impression of Australia; I hoped I was helping. Most probably his family had lost relatives in the war in Afghanistan. Ali may have even seen a bomb or a mine go off, seen people killed—all that before they had made it across the border to Pakistan where they may have been looked down upon and mistreated.

Yes, Australia would be truly the Land of the Free to families like this, the Great Southern Land of new beginnings where they could be safe, if the government let them stay. Ali's eyes were large and round; there was a scar above his left eye. He looked so innocent but I knew he would've seen more than I had, suffered more than me. I hoped he didn't remember it and this would be a happy new world for him.

Dad took over once we arrived at the Migrant Centre. It was difficult prising Ali off me but Dad's fluent Dari helped. Elly wanted to stay to meet his parents but I couldn't get home quickly enough. And once I'd thrown myself on the bed, I couldn't stop crying. This time it was just like Elly in the Teddy Bear Shop. I never cry like that but I couldn't control the sobs from bursting out like the electric shocks that start someone's heart again.

I guess I was crying for Ali at first, for all he must have gone through, his family and how sad they must be to leave Afghanistan in the state it's in, yet so full of hope in coming to Australia, hope in the new life they'd make for their kids.

It wasn't long before I was crying for myself. Mum and Dad had done that too: come back for us so we could have choices in life, live the life we wanted. Everyone seemed to think that could be done in Australia. Suddenly I realised it was true, but only true if you made it so. It would become true for Ali's family; they'd work, they'd enrich Australia and make it a better place. Couldn't I too? Sure, there was a lot wrong, but no place was perfect. It would certainly be less perfect if we kept pulling it down like I was. I could choose to make it home.

Ali's family had chosen and they couldn't go back. They would make Australia their home even though they would feel strange at first. Could I do any less when I was born here? When I was an Australian?

I awoke early the next morning to the sounds of the men stirring on the verandah and in the room next door. If I put a single foot out of the bed, I knew Rushda would wake, so I turned over carefully and glanced across to Suneel's mother.

'You are awake, little one?' Wasn't that what Suneel had called me or was that a dream? His mother was smiling at me. She must have known all along; they must have decided between them that I would be the one. But why? While everyone was quiet and I had her to myself I thought I'd never find a better time to find out.

'Rushda told me last night that I am like Suneel's mother. What did she mean?'

There was a silence from the older woman as if she were weighing up exactly what to say. I wouldn't be offended. I knew we didn't look alike. How could we? Maybe something in our personalities? I was totally unprepared for her answer when she finally did give it.

'I am not the true mother of Suneel.'

I sat up straighter on the bed. 'What do you mean?'

'It is an old story.' She sounded weary. 'I have been Suneel's mother ever since his birth but I did not birth him.'

'He's adopted?' I must admit the thought had crossed my mind when I first saw those green eyes of his.

'Nay, child. His mother died in childbirth here in the village. The khan, my husband, is his true father. Soon after, I became his wife and I became Suneel's mother.'

Did I dare ask? I barely whispered, 'What was she like, his mother?'

There was a sigh. I wasn't sure whether it was in resignation or of missing someone she once loved. 'She was like you. She was full of dreams and aspirations. She was going to help the world. One day she came here on her own, exploring, at one with herself and the world and her God. Yes, she was just like you. She was English too.'

I sank back on the bed, shocked, but my curiosity was aroused.

'What happened?'

'The khan chose her, of course. What did you expect? She was a jewel. They were very happy.'

I was quiet awhile but Suneel's mother continued. 'When Suneel comes today there will be dancing and he will publicly choose you. Later, privately, he will ask you to marry him. You should accept.'

'What about my faith?'

'You will find Suneel very tolerant of your beliefs. We Kalasha are not Muslim.'

'What about my parents?' Why was I suddenly thinking up objections? So they'd be swept away and I'd know my heart decision was right?

'It will all be arranged. They will come and give their blessing also.'

I suppose my parents couldn't forcibly take me with them if I wanted to stay, but I couldn't imagine they'd be overjoyed that I wouldn't finish high school.

'Could I still study if I stayed? I mean, go to university?'

'Anything is possible,' was the enigmatic reply.

Then she added softly, 'Choose wisely, child. Risk happiness.'

15

On the weekend I went to see Yasmeen. I needed some warm fuzzies and she was excellent at handing them out. I still hadn't spoken to Danny and I knew if he didn't initiate a meeting, I would soon. But I didn't feel like thinking about him just then, so I put on a shalwar qameez, enjoying the satisfying swish of the material against my legs.

Dressing like that made me feel beautiful, well-dressed. I guess there was more to it that I wouldn't have been able to explain, but the clothes, the Urdu language and knowing Yasmeen's family customs made me feel accepted in their circle. I guess it was like the girls at school dressing alike in the same label jeans and shoes and speaking the same slang to be part of the 'in' group.

Yasmeen was getting ready to go out later on. She always began early, but as usual had time for me. I sat on her bed, watching her put on layer upon layer of mascara and Pakistani black kohl, pulling down her bottom eyelid as she ran the steel kohl stick across the inside white ridge. I flinched as if it were my eyelid feeling the cold steel, but she was obviously used to it; mothers even put it on their newborns in Pakistan. I grinned, thinking what Australian nurses would have to say about that.

'Yasmeen?'

She screwed the filigree steel stopper into the kohl bottle and turned to face me.

'Ji?' I loved her little Pakistani 'yes'. It always made her eyes dance, her face shine and me feel wanted. Her full attention was on me now but for once I was nervous. I had to find out how far her acceptance of me went; how long I would remain her friend if I didn't keep all her rules?

'Would you ever wear a short skirt, Yasmeen?'

'Of course not.' I don't know why I'd started asking the questions; I knew the answers. I couldn't back out either for, judging by the interested look on her face, she could tell I had something on my mind. I just blurted it out the way Basil gets rid of surplus chicken skin at dinnertime.

'What if you saw me with a boy? What would you think?'

'Jameela, you are not Pakistani. It is your custom to fall in love before you marry, to marry whom you choose. If you find a nice boy, that is good. Although I do think many people here go too far.'

'You mean single mothers, our high abortion rate?' Suddenly I could think of numerous issues in our culture that Yasmeen would see as problems and I thought she would readily add to them, but she didn't. Instead she came to sit beside me on the bed.

'Jameela, no culture has the only correct way. We have many rules to safeguard ours, for we know that a society that is morally weak will quickly be swallowed up by another, but there are things in ours I don't like also.' She surprised me into silence.

'Take circumcision for girls—I wouldn't want that to happen to me. And because of our strict rule system there are many occasions when those rules are forced on others. I have friends in Pakistan who are married to men they never saw beforehand. Some never had a chance to say "no". At least, my father will ask me if I desire the match.'

'You'd never go out with a guy though, would you?' What a stupid question. The look on her face couldn't have been more withering if I'd asked her if she'd murder her mother.

'Never. Besides, I know whom I shall marry already. There would be no point.' I understood but I couldn't help thinking friendship with a guy could be nice; they have a different way of looking at things from girls. Then I thought of Danny and remembered how much more easily it could go wrong too, because there was always that other dimension: the chemistry side of it.

Yasmeen put her arm around me. 'You look beautiful in our clothes, you wear them well. You know our customs and my parents would not mind Shehzad marrying a girl like you. But you are not Pakistani.' She was meaning to be helpful, so why did I suddenly feel so stripped and wretched?

'We all have to find our own place wherever we are and be true to it. We can treat you as a sister and you are my dearest friend, but you do not believe what we do. Deep down you listen to a different voice and you will never be one of us as you are part of your own culture.'

'Sometimes I feel more Pakistani than Australian.' I hoped I didn't sound stubborn but I could feel something being ripped away from me and I wanted to dig my fingernails in to hang on. 'I didn't feel like that in Pakistan. There I knew who I was.'

Yasmeen took off her chiffon scarf then and held it over my eyes. 'Tell me what you see.'

'Everything has a red haze over it.'

'And the curtains? What colour are they?'

'Red.' I pulled the scarf away. The curtains weren't red. I stared at the flimsy white scrim moving gently at the window.

'If you looked through your own scarf, everything would be a different colour, would it not?'

I picked up the end. She was right; the curtains looked as if they'd been left in the blue rinse Shuhila used to soak our sheets in. I didn't say anything. I felt I was going to hear something I hadn't asked for.

'At the moment you are wearing two pairs of glasses and the colours are neither one thing nor the other—not pure. If you looked at those curtains through both scarves at once they would be purple.'

Instantly, I knew where she was heading. 'But I don't want to stop thinking like you.'

'You do not need to, but you must learn to choose your moments. It is like wearing glasses with silk attached. We have learned to take one pair off and put on another in a matter of moments. But predominantly we have one set on.'

'Rosina has chosen to wear another?'

She nodded. 'It is possible to understand two different ways of thinking but you have to choose which one should take the lead or you will always be confused. You will always fall between two worlds, wanting to be in the other place when you are not, always yearning for something else, your soul restless and alien in both places.'

My eyes were watering but she was tender as she continued. 'I tell you this because I love you and I have watched Rosina also. You are trying so hard to be like us. You do not have to. We love you as you are because you understand us and accept us. It is enough. If you want to wear our clothes because you like them, that is good. But please do not feel you must on our account. If you are out with a boy at the movies, please do not feel you must rush the other way. It is your custom. We understand.'

'Did Rosina tell you?'

'Ji, but my parents do not know that Rosina was there that day so please do not mention it.' I shook my head, astounded that she'd known all along, yet her manner had never changed towards me.

'When I first came, Jameela, I was finishing high school also. Then I realised it was as though the Australian girls in my class were seeing life in an entirely different colour from me, and when people see things in a different light, communication is difficult. I had to learn I could not be exactly like them, that I saw things differently. In time, I came to see how they understood things as well.

'Maybe it is more difficult in your case, for you can see

through our glasses and theirs at the same time, getting a different perspective from us all.' She hugged me then. I sure needed it. In some way, I felt as if I'd been taken apart piece by piece yet I still felt whole. I could only hope I was all there and no bits were missing.

'Choose which world to live in, Jameela, and visit the other often.'

That afternoon all the girls had washed, redone each other's hair and put on their shell headdresses. Rushda had taken over the details of my life so well I didn't need to do anything for myself.

'We go to river now,' she stated as the other girls bustled around. It sounded like an invitation just to me, yet all the girls were heading down to a large grassy, flat area guarded by huge gnarled and ancient-looking trees. Suneel's mother walked beside me.

'Our dances were once kept only as celebrations to nature, the change of seasons—a celebration of life, one could say. Today, it will be so again.'

'Isn't it always?'

'Nay. Sadly many people have found how interesting our little valleys are. Once our culture claimed a million people, now there are only three thousand of us in these valleys. To survive, we often dance for payment, so tourists can see how we used to be.' I could sense the bitterness and the shame in her tone.

'But Suneel wants to change all that. He has ideas of starting a weaving factory, creating rugs and blankets with goat hair. They do it in parts of the Arab world. Our people would be making their own money and not be at the mercy of the materialistic revolution that is raping this whole country.' I didn't answer. It sounded too serious for me to comment.

The girls were forming a circle. Suneel's mother beckoned me to link my arm with hers as Rushda was doing with my other arm. The men were further off and a teenage boy carrying a huge roughly-made drum stepped into the centre. The girls were giggling. There were young children as well, the little girls in miniature headdresses like the older girls.

The steady beat of the drum began, echoing my heart, as the girls sang a high pitched chant while their feet slowly and rhythmically stepped round the circle.

I found the slowness of the dance deeply moving, not only because I was sneaking looks at the other side of the river, watching for Suneel to appear, but because it made me feel one with the lush green surroundings, at peace and thankful for the beautiful world.

A sigh broke out from the chanters; the drummer shifted beat. Suneel was walking down towards us, flanked by his father and the village men. Like the other men he wore traditional clothes: the baggy trousers and long shirt with a rolled lambswool cap set back on his sunlit head.

The drummer stopped and the chanting died down as Suneel entered the circle. Then the drum beat again, slower than before as Suneel walked around the inside of the chanters' circle, until he stopped with his back towards me. The drum rolled, Suneel turned, his right hand stretched out. Without thinking, I put my hand in his, the way any Westerner will instinctively do when they see an open palm.

Everyone was clapping and laughing but I didn't feel as if I'd accepted a proposal, though I felt wanted. Rushda was practically bursting with pride and mirth as if she'd been picked herself. Wouldn't she have liked to be chosen? Yet there was no jealousy in her smile. I had a lot to learn about acceptance and oneness from a person like Rushda, who lived the ancient teaching that what was good for all was best for one.

I wondered if I could live like that—like Rushda, like them. What if Suneel decided to take another wife when I was forty? Not being Muslim, he probably wouldn't, but there'd be something else I didn't understand.

Suneel couldn't have looked more pleased if he'd been on a prancing white stallion with my scarf on the end of his sword and a dead dragon at his feet. It might be exciting to help him with these people. It'd be social work, like Dad did. Yet was it really for me? In that moment, I wasn't sure.

16

'I didn't want to come back.' Dad was grinding coffee beans. He liked to do it by hand, turning the wrought-iron handle on the wheel slowly, smelling the fragrance as the beans gave up their pungent treasure. Even Mum preferred to do many things by hand and crushed garlic in a huge wooden mortar with a pestle she'd brought from Pakistan. It was probably one of the reasons no one else's curries came close to hers for flavour.

'What do you mean?' I was finally getting a 'deep and meaningful' with Dad. It was going well. I'd heard something new already, for I'd thought I was the only one that didn't want to return. 'You chose to come back, didn't you?'

'Yes, we chose. But that doesn't mean my heart was in it.'

I leaned closer to the grinder, my eyes shut. Freshly ground coffee was therapeutic.

'I was happy there, doing what I'd been trained to do, what I thought I was meant to. Don't get me wrong, I wanted the best for you kids and that's why we returned. Your mother wanted to come back.'

'She was happy there too, wasn't she?'

'Yes, but she can change midstream quicker than me.

Once she sees the reason for a plan, off she goes. That's why she's coped better. If it wasn't for your mother holding this family together these past six months …'

I could've said, 'Dad, you've been fine,' but we'd both know it was a fib just to make him feel better.

'I'm glad you're feeling better, Dad. I didn't know what to say to you. Some days you were just like Basil with his tail caught in the door, roaring one minute and your head in the corner the next.'

'Was I really like that?' Poor Dad. On the one hand he looked as if he wished I hadn't been so graphic, yet he also seemed pleased we were talking at last. He tapped ground coffee out of the drawer of the grinder. My taste buds were hoping he'd make coffee with it.

'I felt displaced when we returned. I wasn't expecting that. I thought it would be easy, because I knew everything here. But I'd changed so much. I felt like a blundering idiot every time I tried to do anything. Things here had changed. I felt as though I didn't belong, yet I was born here.'

'Did you feel like that too? I thought you were just missing Pakistan.'

'I couldn't have put it into words then, I suppose. Maybe we should have commiserated together.'

'Mum seemed fine.'

'Yep. But there were times that she didn't tell you kids about. Did you know she walked into a supermarket, walked around for two hours and came home with nothing?'

I shook my head. I couldn't imagine Mum doing that at all.

'There were too many choices. It just got too much.'

'Like Elly in the Teddy Bear Shop.' And me with the music and the movies, and Danny, and school.

'Is it worth it, Dad? All the pain and confusion?'

He put his arm around me then. 'Of course it is. We're all doing much better now. Give us another year or two and we'll all be totally adjusted. But that experience of living in a different culture from your own is one of the most enriching things that can happen to a person. You have a different perspective on life from the one you would have had if you'd been brought up here.'

I got the coffee mugs out to trigger Dad's brain into making coffee. It worked; his hand reached for the filter papers. Since he was getting introspective, I decided to throw something at him that had been bothering me all year.

'Dad, who do you think I am?'

He grinned, the 'I'm twenty-five years older than you' type of grin. 'That seems to be the catchphrase today, doesn't it? We never thought about it much when we were young.' I must have looked impatient for he swung me around on the stool so we were face-to-face.

'I'll tell you who you are, if you so desperately want to know. You are Jaime Richards—maybe a bit different from the usual run-of-the-mill kid, but that's what makes you Jaime. Don't knock it. It just happens to be the reason why you're so special.'

I don't know whose eyes got mistier, but it was so good to have him back in one piece. Even through all those years in boarding school and the quality holidays we had, making every moment count, he'd never said anything quite like that.

Later, Suneel and I had been left alone, if one could call it that. There were still people in view but at a distance. Suneel began talking about the valleys of the Kalasha; there were three but the valley of Rumbur was definitely his passion.

'It's pathetic how our culture is being diluted. We've lived through countless invasions, we're the only community in the whole of Pakistan to have held out against Islam. It wasn't smiled upon either, but we survived.'

He grinned then, although nothing seemed funny. 'Now we've come smack up against Western twenty-first century materialism and the four-wheel-drive.' He made it sound as if he'd been alive since Alexander the Great. He made me see his vision, made me almost feel the fire in his belly as he outlined ways he'd achieve his goals.

'Do you see this?' He pointed to the scar that ran down his cheek. My head nodded; I'd wondered about it. 'I was beaten at school for not becoming Muslim. The older boy had a knife. He said he'd cut my heart out, then I'd be sure to go to Paradise. As it was, I was lost, he said. But I knew even at that age what I must do, what I must be.' He stepped closer to me as his voice became softer but the passion didn't leave his tone.

'I want to save our valleys, our way of life, our

traditions before it's all washed away in a tide of plastic bags, TV sets and long-life milk.'

For the first time I wondered if he was prone to exaggerate. Then I remembered this would end up being a proposal and tried to gather my thoughts together.

'Little one.' He took off his cap and held it across his chest in the humble fashion in which he'd apologised to me in the jewellery shop. Was it only two weeks ago? 'Please become my wife. As soon as I saw you, I knew it would be you. We can do this together. I know we can.'

My breathing stopped a second as if my heart was taking stock of life and deciding whether to carry on. I'd waited for this moment, dreamed of it; thought of nothing else for the past few days. What could I say?

I stared up at him standing there, hope mixed with confidence in his eyes as he waited. His smile, now tender, would grow to one of love and passion for me, not just for the valleys. Life with him would never be boring; it would have excitement, meaning and purpose but would it be my purpose, my life?

Then, I knew. I turned away for a moment to pull my thoughts in order before I faced him. 'Suneel, I'm honoured, but I'm so sorry. However much I would grow to love you and your people, I can't stay. This is not my country, its ways are not mine, your people not mine.'

He bent to interrupt me, but I put out my hand to keep him at bay, so I could think clearly.

'My parents are leaving for Australia in a few months. Please understand. There are things I haven't done. I want to go to university. I want to know my family, my country. I want to find out where I fit in the whole world, not just here.'

'Jameela—' The anguish in his eyes was a terrible thing to see. His hands shook as he brought them up to his chest. 'You must not do this. It is written in here that you are the one. You will love me. Please do not be afraid.'

'Love is not the problem.' I daren't tell him I cared already, for maybe he'd try more effective persuasion. 'Please understand. Your people will never accept me, not totally. I'd always be the foreign princess, the one that came from afar, who was different. Every time there is a war or some political crisis with extremists, you would have to hide me. I won't always be able to stand at your side. Don't you see? We have different visions. We look down a different path.'

As I stood there watching him trying to wrap self-respect around himself and draw up extra strength from inside, I knew I couldn't stay. Sooner or later I'd wish I'd chosen differently. All the same, I hated to say those things. I wanted to hug him, say I cared, say it wasn't because of him, but I dared not touch him. If I did, I knew I'd forget all that I'd said as I remembered clearly what it felt like to be shielded from death by his warmth and to feel my heart jolt in a happy sort of pain when he was standing close.

He closed his eyes. At first I was surprised he

didn't argue further; then I began thinking of his mother and the people of the village. They'd be happily expecting my positive answer. Hadn't I put my hand in his at the dancing? Then a frightening thought occurred to me. Would he force me to stay? He was quiet for what seemed a long time until he finally spoke.

'Jameela, I too am sorry. Maybe I expected too much, and too soon.'

Suddenly I was sobbing; I felt Suneel's arms come round me, tentatively, as though years of abstinence made them rusty and stiff.

'There is no need to weep,' I heard him say. 'Your parents will come and take you. Everything will be arranged.'

'But I'm so sorry. You had a dream and I ruined it.'

He held me away from him then so I could see his face—sad, but still protective of me. 'That is not your concern. We cannot be responsible for making other people's dreams come true.' He held me again then. I was sure he wasn't supposed to, especially after I'd said 'no' but it was almost as if he needed just a tiny taste of what it would have been like.

'Do not forget, little one, this country, the way you have been raised as one of us. It has shaped the way you see the world. It is part of you. Do not deny it.'

'I'll never forget, Suneel, not anything.' Especially not you, my heart cried, but how could I say things that would only make us feel worse? How could I explain that in loving him I could still leave? I doubted he'd understand.

'Jameela, we will never find another moment alone so I will say goodbye now. May you live long and your soul find rest in your country, not toss like treetops in a storm.'

'Thank you.' It was useless trying to stop the tears rolling down my face. 'Goodbye, Suneel. I hope you find your dream.'

He smiled faintly and touched my face as he did in the dream, as though it had to last forever.

Then he kissed the tips of his own wet fingers. 'And you, yours.'

The tears were dropping onto my hands. Suneel, my dear Pakistan. I'd never said goodbye. I guess because I didn't want to go. My body had stubbornly walked up those steps to the plane without turning around to wave. The inside part of me kept saying, 'I'll be back' and I didn't realise that leaving was also a kind of loving.

17

Danny had been on my mind a lot but I still didn't feel like talking to him at school. What if it took two hours and we missed lessons? It just seemed easier to do nothing. As time went on, though, I knew there was more behind our misunderstanding than his being piqued at not being in my story.

That Saturday I was about to ring him when he rolled up in his cousin's car, armed with a picnic that his little sisters had put together. Mum was only too pleased to see him. She ordered her life to achieve a certain level of peace and harmony and didn't rest until everybody close to her felt as calm as herself.

'Take as long as you like,' she whispered to me as I went out the door. She probably thought I was still sorting through the dross of settling in here. I guess it was part of it in a way, but I couldn't help thinking a problem like Danny could happen any time, any place. It couldn't all be because of me.

It's funny how a trait can be so much a part of a person that you don't truly notice it until it's gone. When we were walking into the park, I couldn't get over how

Danny seemed to have no dance left. His body used to kind of move as a whole. Now just his legs walked; just his arm reached over to pick up a plastic cup and his eyes only watched; they didn't get involved like they used to.

I thought I'd better say something more meaningful than how nice the day was and all the other mundane things we'd said in the car.

'I'm sorry I didn't ring. I was going to today.'

'That's cool. I couldn't either.' I knew his 'couldn't' didn't mean he'd had no time or was too busy. He sounded like I felt when I didn't want to think about a subject because I couldn't handle it yet. I watched him pour the Coke. He seemed smaller. Could a guy lose weight that quickly? It'd only been a few weeks.

'Danny, I'm sorry.' I leaned over just as he looked up. It was like his pupils opened wide and I could see right inside, a private place just for me, except I didn't feel I had the right to look.

'And the story? That Pakistani guy?'

'It's all finished. None of it was true anyway.' I knew now why he'd cared so much about that stupid story. Once I'd finished it, I could see it all: the look on Danny's face as he swung round from the computer screen, the hurt edge in his voice.

'I'm sorry I called the story crap.'

'That hurt.'

'So did I.' His hand found mine. 'But I didn't mean it about the story itself. What I read was great—you should write more—but I could see between the lines, that's all.'

He stood then and pulled me up.

'Come on. Let's walk a bit. It sounded like some world you'd made up to escape to and I didn't think you had to do that.' He turned to me then. 'Wasn't I helping?'

'Of course you were. I wouldn't have survived the first weeks at school without you.' Then I added, 'I'm sorry you weren't in the story but it was about Pakistan.' Did he buy that? Or did he understand, like Mr Bolden, that it was about now, too?

He didn't answer for a while but when he did it felt as if a breeze had suddenly sprung up and pushed me backwards.

'I was the one—' He didn't finish but I knew what he meant.

He, not Suneel. How could I write about a fantasy guy when a real one was ready and willing? Maybe that was the problem. I didn't think I could handle him saying those sorts of things yet so I explained about the story. Yasmeen's words readily came to mind.

'I just felt between two worlds, like their borders were shrinking and I was going to get squashed in the crack. I was just trying to crawl out, to unjumble the mess.'

He stopped walking then and drew me to face him. 'Maybe you are between two worlds like you say, but look at yourself for once in the real light. All you can think of is whether you're fitting in. But Jaime, it doesn't matter. You're beyond borders.'

I blinked. What a phrase! He seemed pleased with it. I was glad; it was the first thing he'd looked pleased about all morning.

'Look, no other Australian girl has come into our house, enjoyed herself and been so totally accepted by my parents as you have. Take your friend, Yasmeen. Could any other girl in your class talk about the things she does, understand her accent, wear her clothes?'

An image of Debra, demure in Pakistani clothes and head scarf failed to come to mind. 'I guess not.'

'Jaime, you could identify with anybody. Being part of two worlds is weird, maybe it's difficult at times, but it makes you more interesting and surely you have a bigger outlook on things than most of the kids at school.'

'But sometimes people make me feel like I've flown in from another planet.'

'So what? That's not them doing that, it's you letting them.' He almost poked me with his finger. 'It's what you feel in here that counts. If you feel fine, then no crap from the other kids is going to ruin your day. Besides, if you feel an alien here you'll feel one there too. I've been to Greece. I know.'

I nodded. I'd already worked that one out with the help of Suneel. I sighed. Then Danny's hands were on my shoulders. 'Jaime, I loved you, you know.' It was the other half of the sentence he didn't finish before. The past tense didn't fool me either. I knew it was insurance in case I laughed.

What do you say? It was like he'd unzipped all his skin and his insides were about to tumble out and I could save him with four small words: I love you too.

I almost did it just to zip him up again, but Suneel's story had taught me more than just coping in a new world. 'Danny, I do care for you, I think I always will, but it's different. Sooner or later you'd expect something I couldn't do—not the way I was brought up. It wouldn't work.'

He looked as if he'd interrupt but I wanted to explain. 'I need you so much, but as a friend. Someone to hug me when I need it, listen to me. You're the one at school who knows the most about me. You know what I've been through. You showed me stuff. I'd like to be there for you too, but can't we call ourselves "friends"? Is there such a thing here in Australia?'

It took a while, but he managed to wipe off the exposed, ragged look that had taken over his face. He gave me his old 'that's cool' grin in the offhand way of his which I knew by then wasn't offhand at all.

'Well, that's better than I expected, I guess. So you do care?' I nodded. Vigorously.

'You know if you don't go out with me, I'll go out with other girls?' His tone implied 'won't that bother you?'

I tried to grin in a fair imitation of his. 'That's cool.'

He sort of smiled and sighed at the same time as he drew me against him and held me. 'I'll try, Jaime. Just give me a bit of time, OK?' There was a lot I didn't understand about guys, like why he'd need time and for what, but I nodded anyway.

He stood back then. 'If you don't see me for a while, don't worry. I won't have forgotten.'

I just nodded again for I knew if I tried to talk words

wouldn't come out; something else would.

He kissed me then. It was the last time he kissed me on my mouth and I could taste the salt of unreached dreams.

18

'Hi, Jaime. Whatcha doing?'

I couldn't believe this solicitous inquiry was from Kate. Things did seem to have changed though I couldn't pinpoint what in particular. Maybe I was just getting used to the scene at school but I seemed to get nagged less. I found myself answering her in language that would have been Martian to me six months before.

'Just hanging. Got heaps of work to do, though.'

Kate grimaced in sympathy. Even she was getting into some serious study. 'The year's going too fast, hey?'

I nodded to her, wondering how time can affect relationships. At the beginning of the year, I couldn't have imagined myself passing the time of day with her like this. She still swore so badly that I could see flames of hellfire hover above her head, and Debra practically meditated on jeans and sneakers labels, yet the more I used their words—like 'cool', 'hot' and 'heaps'—the more they seemed to understand me. It was weird, for I didn't think I was talking about different things from before.

True to his word, after a few weeks Danny talked to me again at lunch. It was like when I first came but more relaxed. Neither of us felt any pressure that we had to spend time together. I could tell him anything without that feeling of having to tone it down because of his interest in me. Once he asked my opinion on a story he was writing for Year 12 English. That made me smile.

'You've taught me something, you know,' he said that time. I must have looked surprised for he grinned a bit self-consciously. 'Yeah, that there's more to a relationship than doing it. I'm sorry if I crowded you or anything.'

'But you never tried anything.' Was I so naive that a guy could make a move on me and I didn't even realise?

'Maybe not but it was on my mind a lot.'

'Thanks.' I don't know if either of us knew what I said 'thanks' for but it seemed the right thing to say.

When I first saw Danny with Vasa, I must admit I felt a twang of 'that could have been me' but it soon passed when I saw how she looked at him. I'd never looked at him like that. She was Orthodox, went to the Catholic school, wore her hair long and was very attractive. She didn't look the type to climb out of windows at night and I sincerely wished him the best.

I was still standing outside the classroom when Sara and some of her friends (who were now mine as well) turned up, bags over their shoulders. It reminded me of how Afghan freedom fighters carry their assault rifles. At times I'd get flashes like that, of a world so remote from the scene I was in. Mr Bolden was there before we could get into a deep conversation. He was never late for class.

'So glad you finished the story, Jaime,' were his opening words when I went to his desk. 'It was such a good ending.' To any of the others it would sound like the usual encouraging stuff he'd say about their work, but to me it was as if he thought I'd been about to jump off the roof of the Festival Theatre and I'd walked out of the lift into his arms instead.

'Welcome to Australia,' was all he said then. His eyes were bright and I smiled in surprise. It did feel as if I'd recently arrived. How did he know? He'd understood where Danny hadn't, but then Mr Bolden had been reading all my private thoughts for the past six months. Maybe no one else knew quite as much about me as Mr Bolden. He cleared his throat. 'Jaime, that story served a purpose but I'd like to see you write more when you have time. Just for the sake of writing. Maybe a novel. Would you think about that?'

'Sure, Mr Bolden. And thanks.'

That afternoon, just before I reached the bus stop, a car pulled up behind me at the kerb. This time I wasn't scared; there were kids everywhere. I heard Kate's indrawn breath before I saw the blue front door open for me and recognised my name. I waved at the girls as I hopped into Blake's car. Poor Kate. She didn't even look jealous, just stunned like a rabbit caught in high beam.

'I hope you don't mind my picking you up like this, but I tried to catch you at school today.'

I grinned and hoped I didn't look as stupefied as Kate. My curiosity grew, for he didn't rush to tell me what he wanted. He'd never gone out of his way to find me before, not since that time in the library.

'Do you know our tradition in the school of having a Year 12 dinner before the exams start?'

I nodded. Since the Year 11s were invited too, it was all the girls were talking about lately: what they'd wear, who'd do their hair.

'Well, we always have a Year 11 to give a speech, sort of send us off into the wide, wide world.' He grinned across at me. I hadn't heard about that bit. I realised I hadn't said anything and unsuspecting, I plunged in. 'That sounds a great idea,' I blurted out. Then I wished I hadn't.

He smiled his Coke ad smile. 'I'm glad you think so.' Uh oh.

'Because you've been nominated to do the speech for this year.'

'Me? Why me? I haven't been here long enough.'

'Mr Bolden seems to think you'll do a great job and I happen to agree with him.'

Mr Bolden. I should have guessed. Teachers get to sit in on student council meetings and no doubt put in their ten cents' worth.

'So Mr Bolden put my name forward.' I was rummaging through my mind how to get out of it gracefully when Blake's next comment floored me.

'Actually, it was Danny Dimitriadis.'

'Danny?'

'Yep. He said you were a gutsy babe who'd have something cool to say.'

'Danny said that? What did everyone else say?'

'They all agreed you could do it.'

'But they don't know me.'

'They know Danny, they know me.' He grinned across at me then. 'Stop trying to get out of it. You'll do a good job.'

I fell silent, thinking fast. To have faith put in me like that when I didn't think I was well liked was hard to fathom. Blake had told me, in this very car those months ago, that life would get better. What had changed? Was it only me?

19

Yasmeen had invited me to the mosque and a picnic afterwards to celebrate Pakistan's Day of Independence. I hadn't seen her for a while and when I turned up at her place in long top and pants with matching scarf from the local Indian shop she hugged me.

'It is so good to see you, Jameela. It has been weeks since we last met.'

Even in Australia, I was thinking with an inside grin, Pakistanis can love you so much that you feel guilty when you've been too busy to visit them. I'm sure Yasmeen didn't mean to make me feel bad but just wanted me to know I was missed. I started in on the expected excuses, justifying why I hadn't been.

'I've had so much homework to do. Third term's nearly gone. I think of you all the time, though.' Yasmeen grinned at that as we made our way to their van.

The mosque was deceptively small. Situated on a side street with its minaret rising above the surrounding rooftops, the size of the courtyard inside came as a total surprise. Only men knelt in the actual mosque area while women, many from Indonesia in white robes and scarves, knelt in perfect lines in the outside courtyard. All Yasmeen's Pakistani friends sat in a room that seemed to be assigned for child minding.

'In Pakistan women do not go to the mosque at all,' Yasmeen whispered as I strained to hear her above the babble of hundreds of voices. 'So we do not take an active part here either. We like to pray privately at home.'

My presence wasn't as big a novelty as I thought it might be. In the courtyard, there were a few white Australian guys and in the room with us were some Anglo-Australian women, holding on their laps beautiful children with large brown eyes and light brown skin.

Yasmeen leaned closer again. 'Most of these ladies only come when it's a special day, like Eid or today.' I looked around. It was my first time too.

'My father comes every Friday, Shehzad rarely because of school.'

I nodded in affirmation for I too had to get special permission to take time out of school. The teachers didn't seem to mind but Mr Bolden said I had to write a report.

Rosina was on the other side of me. I wondered how they'd got her there. She had her lips pursed in an 'I didn't want to come' pout. She ignored her mother who sighed every time she glanced across at her daughter's naked head and neck.

Just then a small boy came to stand in front of me, his brown eyes looking up at me from under his dark curly fringe. I gave a little squeal of pleasure as I bent over, arms wide.

'Ali, how nice to see you.' He climbed onto my knee, knowing he was welcome even though he couldn't understand my English words. I spoke in Urdu.

'How are you, Ali?'

'Teik hai, fine,' he answered with a solemn little lift of his head. His mother came looking for him soon after, a young attractive Afghan who spoke English with an educated Kabuli accent.

'Thank you so much. You found Ali.'

I grinned. It was as though she was thanking me for that first time all those weeks ago. When I asked her how she was settling in, it was the Eastern smile of acceptance that spread across her face, lighting up the hope in her eyes.

'There are many things different here and we miss friends and family but we are happy and safe. There are no bombs or mines. My husband is not in jail.' She stroked Ali's forehead as she spoke and I wondered again about his scar.

'What did you do in Kabul?' I wasn't just making conversation. I knew what it felt like to come from another place and no one be interested; to be unable to exorcise the memories, good or bad, so that they got bottled up and grew out of all proportion to what was real.

'I was studying in university when it was bombed. After that education stopped for women. My husband was a teacher. He taught Persian language and history.'

We both fell silent. How on earth would he ever find a job here? I tried to sound encouraging. 'Could he teach that at university here?'

She shook her head. 'We were told he must do another course of study here to get a teaching degree. But,' and then she gave a heavy sigh, 'it would be too difficult with the children.'

I stared at her without anything to say. Dad would say 'another brilliant guy driving a taxi because his expertise wasn't recognised.'

She was speaking again. 'Cousins of ours own a fish and chip business. We will help them for a while.'

Just then a voice from the loud speaker began leading the prayers in ancient Arabic. The beautiful chants echoed across the courtyard as hundreds of believers stood, knelt and prostrated themselves in unison, their lips moving in devotion to a great and merciful God. I guess such a mass of people bowing was an impressive sight and would move the hearts of those who had an empty shape in their souls, but I wondered what it truly meant to those who were there.

When I had told Mr Bolden I was going to the mosque with Yasmeen, he'd looked bothered, as if I might not be sure who I was again. But I told him not to worry, that I was just showing friendship to Yasmeen.

The sermon began and the women who'd covered their heads for the prayers pulled off their scarves and rearranged them about their necks. I copied them. Rosina sat resolute throughout, her face saying louder than words what she was thinking. Then I did hear her murmuring under her breath. It sounded a lot like, 'This is such crap.'

I was genuinely shocked and hoped I'd misheard. For after all, this religion was extremely important to her family and if anyone said something like that in Pakistan, there could be a terrible punishment. People were jailed there for blasphemy, many on death row.

She turned to me then. I almost drew back at the force with which she moved. 'Why are you here? You don't have to listen to this.'

How could I explain that it didn't touch me other than having respect for someone else's beliefs?

She misunderstood my silence. 'Are you becoming Muslim?' She almost spat it out and it made me think of Debra.

Rosina was serious for once so I answered her in kind. 'Islam means everything to people like Yasmeen but I'd rather have a relationship with God without having to keep a heap of rules. I like being loved for who I am, whether I deserve it or not.'

She looked surprised, as though she'd expected me to be jumping thoughtlessly onto the Eastern bandwagon. But I'd learnt that although there were many religions, each person believed only theirs to be true.

Suddenly Yasmeen was there in front of me and I was being introduced to other Pakistani girls as her friend. It felt like a capital 'F' was in order; she seemed so proud of me. Ali's mum was trying to introduce me to her cousins as well. I'd never be able to remember all the names.

'Come now.' Yasmeen guided me through the crowd. It was worse than the airport when we arrived in January. I could hardly manoeuvre past the joking and excited men without brushing against them, as Yasmeen pulled me by my hand. Children were running about, almost pushing between people's legs to get through. Rosina was behind me; I lost Yasmeen's grip. Then I saw Shehzad.

'Hi, again.' His accent sounded weird in a mosque. He managed to make a small passageway for us to make it out the front gate in one piece.

'Talk about wall-to-wall people.'

'Like the bazaar in Lahore the day before Eid,' Shehzad added. He was right.

'The picnic will not be so crowded—just our friends that were at Fozia's birthday party.' Yasmeen gave me a reassuring smile.

I had to grin. 'Just our friends' could mean thirty families and a whole heap of kids!

20

With interest I watched the food appearing on the folding tables: curries, chicken, rice dishes, flat bread, Coke and modern vacuum flasks filled with milky, sweet tea. As Yasmeen's guest I didn't need to bring food, but I couldn't help wondering if her polite insistence not to bring any was tied with ensuring the meat was halal, properly slaughtered in the name of God. All Yasmeen's friends bought their meat from the mosque or from Muslim butchers.

It took so long for everyone to arrive. Elly would have complained of food deprivation by 3 p.m, but even she would have been impressed by the speed with which the food was transferred onto everyone's plates. A late start meant a quick eat, it seemed. I kept thinking of Elly because she liked the simple things in life, but after what happened next I was glad she wasn't there.

I was on my second piece of tandoori chicken when I first noticed the young guys lounging at a picnic table some distance away. One seemed to be looking my way and it made me feel the way I had at the beginning of the year, as if there was a crow on my shoulder. His hair had been shaved and his bulging black T-shirt and leather vest made him look like a criminal. Some of his mates were talking loudly enough for their words to be heard, about dirty boat people taking over the country.

I hoped no one had heard but I forgot about Yasmeen; she was never far from me. 'It is all right,' she said gently. 'Do not be angry. We are used to it.'

'But it's so rude. If only they knew what you all were like.'

'It would not make any difference. Ignore them.'

I stared at the calm acceptance evident in her face and wondered if Shehzad or the other young men would react the same if they'd heard those words.

Just then one of the male cousins called to Yasmeen. 'We are playing soccer. Come and watch.' Just like guys anywhere; they all like to have the girls watch them. Yasmeen beckoned to Rosina and we followed the boys away from the picnic area and swings to an open part of the park.

By the way Rosina's foot kept jerking whenever the guys kicked the ball, I could tell she wanted to play. She wasn't the only one. We both moved in closer, waiting our chance. We didn't have long to wait; the ball came rolling towards us. Rosina was there before me and kicked it back to one of the guys, Amir, Shehzad's friend. The look on his face was priceless as he lost concentration so that Shehzad took control of the ball. None of the adults were close by and I didn't wait to see what Yasmeen would say; I just followed Rosina further into the game.

I was glad the boys let us keep playing. We were all

much the same age so how could it matter? Suddenly, the ball was heading straight towards me. I got ready to mark it as I'd seen footballers do on TV but it was too high. Yasmeen was shouting, but I swung round to chase it up and stopped dead, paralysed by waves of fear that dumped on me. The ball bounced off a table. Bottles and cans flew as it rolled along the grass to land in front of the black-clad guys.

One of them picked up the ball as they all walked purposely towards us. Maybe there were only three or four of them but it seemed like more. It is true: fear does come in waves, one after the other and I was drowning in it. Yasmeen was pulling me, but I couldn't move. Rosina looked belligerent and either wouldn't move, or like me, couldn't.

I know some men like their beer but I suddenly thought how ridiculous they were, being so upset about a stray football. I still didn't know how much more than spilt beer was at stake. I soon found out.

'So you're a terrorist-lover. Next thing they'll be bombing the park.' The owner of the voice was strolling closer to me like a hunter stalking a fox. I didn't like the way he was staring. He hadn't shaved for ages and his eyes made him look as if he was already undoing my buttons. That thought made me take a step backwards.

'Which one of these smelly wogs are you having it off with?' At this he slapped the hand of the guy next to him and they both practically fell on the ground laughing. Those guys calling the Rasheeds and their friends names was so ludicrous that I found my tongue at last.

'They're not terrorists! Can't you hear what you sound like? You're just picking on them because they're different from you.' Besides, they were the terrorists and I wished I had the nerve to say that too.

'Picking on them, are we?' The speaker turned to his mates. I didn't like the look of his grin. 'We want an apology, see, for losing us all our beer.'

I didn't mind apologising for a mistake. I started to, hoping that would be the end of it. 'Of course, we're—' I didn't get any further for Rosina cut in with 'not sorry'.

'Hey?'

'Are you thick? We're not sorry about your stupid beer. It was an accident.'

They must have been so surprised by Rosina's Australian accent that it floored them for a second, but it didn't end there. Apparently they didn't like the word 'thick'.

It all happened quickly then. One grabbed me—I was the terrorist-lover. Another held Rosina as she tried to kick and squirm out of his grip. I heard the material of my shirt rip just as we were both knocked to the ground. I rolled clear in time to see Shehzad on top of the shaved-head guy, practically bashing his face in. Pakistani guys mature early and even though Shehzad was only seventeen, he was just as big as his opponent. Amir, though younger, was trying to deal with the one that had hold of Rosina, except she was doing a fair job of it herself.

I shouldn't have relaxed. One of the guys who hadn't said anything before suddenly took hold of me and started to shake me. Then he slapped me, all the while saying stuff about teaching me a lesson, that I shouldn't be a wog-lover; they come illegally and take all our jobs. If he didn't have a job, it wasn't hard to work out why. I would have liked to tell him what I really thought of him but I was dizzy and could taste blood in my mouth. I had no fight left.

That was when Shehzad pulled him off and belted him across the mouth. Guys brought up like Shehzad are fed so much stuff about the honour of women. I'd often wondered where he had stood in his family's beliefs; I was seeing it now. I was Yasmeen's friend, which gave me the status of sister, and I'd known of guys in Pakistan who'd kill to save their sisters. I couldn't see Yasmeen and hoped she'd gone for her father. I had to stay, even though I couldn't help and hated to watch.

All the black-clad guys were onto Shehzad and Amir then and it was obvious the younger guys wouldn't be able to hold them off. Besides, the numbers weren't fair. I was sobbing as one of them held Shehzad while another punched him again and again in the head, in the stomach. How could anyone stand so much punishment? Amir was still fighting, but it was in slow motion, as if the thugs knew they'd won and were going to enjoy the game a little longer.

I heard the shouts before Dr Rasheed and the other men arrived to pull the guys off Shehzad. The guy fighting with Amir had already slunk away and Amir was feeling his body gingerly, checking if he was in one piece. Shehzad wasn't even moving. Blood covered his shirt, and his face was hardly recognisable. He lay on the ground, not even groaning, as his father expertly felt over his body for injuries.

'I'm so sorry.' I was openly crying and felt so responsible. If Rosina and I weren't there, maybe it wouldn't have happened. Yasmeen had returned and she hugged me tight.

Amir must have heard what I said for he gave me a wry grin. 'Don't blame yourself, Jameela. They were only using you to make us fight. It would have happened even if you and Rosina weren't here.' He still sounded jaunty through his tiredness and I wondered if it had occured before. I shuddered; I certainly never wanted to go through that again. Soon it was my turn to be inspected by Yasmeen's father. His prognosis included a black eye and bruising but I'd heal.

'Will Shehzad be all right?' I was almost too scared to ask for fear of what I'd be told.

'We will take him to hospital now.' His father's voice was tight. 'There may be internal bleeding. Be careful,' he said suddenly as some of the men lifted Shehzad.

Dad picked me up from the Rasheeds' place. He kept looking at me in the same way Mr Bolden used to in first term. The shock had started to set in by the time we got home and I was a shivering mess. Mum got out the ice pack and extra blankets, saying I had a black eye as good as Andrew's when his sneakers were taken. She was trying to cheer me up. I wished they didn't try so hard. I was fine, really.

Mum sat with me until I felt like talking. Looking back on it, the worst part was watching Shehzad getting beaten just because he was different. Mum kept saying not everyone was like that and I knew it too, but it still made me feel terrified as though nowhere was safe. It made me want to go back to Pakistan on the next flight.

I heard them talking later when they thought I was asleep.

Who could sleep!

'She was doing so well, too. Now this will set her back worse than before.'

They made it sound as if I'd been a real problem. Had I? Their voices became muffled then, but the worried tones couldn't be disguised. That was when I made up my mind. However long it took me to get over this I wouldn't let it beat me. Why let those guys win? Danny had told me, hadn't he? It was what was inside me that counted. It was how I reacted to things that determined the effect they'd have on me. I could choose to let it grind me into dust and wallow in self-pity or rise above it and soar like an eagle in a storm.

21

It seemed to take weeks before Shehzad came out of hospital. Whenever Yasmeen visited him on the weekends, I went too, for I didn't think he or his family would understand if I went by myself. I was beginning to see that although Shehzad wore the best label jeans and sounded more Australian than Danny, he still had a Pakistani way of looking at things when it came to the crunch.

The first time he opened his eyes and smiled at me I got teary with relief. By then I knew it wasn't my fault that Shehzad was beaten up but I was scared he might think so.

'I'm sorry,' was all I could whisper that first time. There was so much I didn't say—sorry, not just for my being there, but for his getting half killed and for what? Because he was dark-skinned, good looking and intelligent? That he would do better in this country than those guys who beat him and they knew it? Or was it just senseless animal instinct of culling out the different ones in the herd?

When I looked at Shehzad's bruises and bandaged stomach, I felt ashamed I was Australian until I remembered I'd seen it happen in Pakistan as well. I sighed. At least our police were trying to stop it.

I said it again in case he hadn't heard. 'Shehzad, I'm so sorry.' He smiled again, slowly, as if his face hurt when he moved it. I felt more encouraged. His eyes were very much alive and he used them in the way Danny would have used his arms. I grinned back, wishing I could touch his hand, but I didn't dare.

'It's cool, Jameela. Don't worry. They were off their faces.'

Shehzad's seemingly easy dismissal of it astounded me. I didn't remember thinking the thugs were so drunk, or was Shehzad just trying to make me feel better?

As I left that day, I found I couldn't deal with the whole thing as quickly or as easily as the Rasheeds' tight-lipped acceptance. For weeks I'd wake suddenly in the early hours, not able to cope with the dream I'd been having, usually of Shehzad, or Rosina and me getting killed.

The dreams gradually subsided, as did the feelings of anger that the thugs seemed to have gotten away with it. I never found out if they were caught or if the Rasheeds had even pressed charges. I told my friends at school about it so they wouldn't keep annoying me with inquiries about my bruises, and Mr Bolden treated me as if I were one of those kids with a blood disorder. He even let me off the report on the mosque.

By the day of the Year 12 dinner I was more myself again. Blake found me in the library putting the final touches to my speech. 'How ya going?'

I grinned. I was becoming more comfortable with him. He'd been so helpful to me and I found sun-drenched blond wasn't as off-putting as I first thought.

'Not nervous, are you?'

'A bit.' Actually I was panic-stricken but who'd admit to that? I'd had a hard time working out what to say to school leavers about the workforce, getting a job, going to university. Blake said I could talk about whatever I wanted, but I needed a straightforward topic to keep my nerves in straight lines. Dad had helped me, but I couldn't understand why they didn't get a teacher to do the speech. As it happened, I needn't have spent so much time on all that research. It all came out differently from what I'd planned.

Contrary to the impression I gave the girls, I did worry about what to wear. I couldn't see myself in one of those low cut or strapless gowns that most of them were wearing. I still found it hard to show that much flesh in public, yet I wanted to look elegant and Western too. Nothing in the shops turned me on so I finally resorted to designing an outfit myself. Yasmeen made it up for me. She could sew a dress just from seeing a picture of it. That never ceased to amaze me.

If she was shocked about the short sleeves, she never said. She just seemed pleased that I'd created an outfit so totally me. When Mrs Rasheed saw the blue silk Western-looking harem pants she smiled. The smile faded abruptly when she saw the flimsy, five-gored dress that went with them but Yasmeen understood. She'd been to school and knew what it was like to try to fit in.

The Abbey restaurant had heritage decor with dim lights, and if I wasn't about to give a speech, I would have truly appreciated it. A band was playing on a raised platform in one corner and I was still wondering if there'd be dancing when Sara found a place for us to sit at a table with some of our Year 11 friends. Danny and Vasa were sitting on the opposite side and Danny gave me one of his special grins as I sat down. Vasa apparently didn't mind his friendship with me. Besides, she looked too self-assured to bother about what other girls thought of her boyfriend. If she was what he used to call 'old worldish', she certainly wasn't mindless, as he'd made Greek girls out to be that night in our kitchen ten months ago.

Kate came over to say 'hi'. I could see Debra sitting at the table next to us. Both girls had on dresses so tight they must have had trouble breathing, and they had brought boyfriends. I saw an image of Mrs Rasheed's face if she were there. A giggle rose right out of my throat but I changed it to a choke just in time. Kate kindly banged me on the back. I told her it was nerves.

'Because of the speech,' I added when she looked blank. Kate always acted as if she never knew what nerves were.

Then I saw Blake. I couldn't get over how interesting he looked in a suit. All I'd ever seen him in were his school uniforms and PE tracksuits. Nor had I realised how much like Suneel he'd become. Or did I put that around the wrong way? To tell the truth, I couldn't remember the real Suneel by then.

Finally, the dreaded moment arrived. There was a break in the music as the band took a break. Apparently, we'd finished dessert. Elly would never understand that I couldn't remember what I'd eaten at the Abbey. Blake started off the evening's entertainment, as he put it. Then Billy and a group of the Year 11 boys did a skit, in the style of Shakespeare, taking off teachers and students without partiality.

I wasn't paying much attention until Billy suddenly came out with 'Oh, good grief! Where are my sunglasses? The grass in Pakistan is too, too green.' Everybody laughed. No one got missed out, so why should I? Then I saw the funny side of it. Had I really sounded like that? No one was being nasty, just joining in the fun. Suddenly I felt like one of them; I didn't need to be treated with kid gloves anymore. I could take what everyone else got and enjoy it for what it was: just ordinary Aussie humour.

Too soon it was my turn. Everyone clapped as I made my way to the microphone. No one looked at me as if I had purple toads on my head; no one stared at my harem pants. Mr Bolden was watching me as if he'd discovered me in a jungle and I was about to utter my first word ever. Danny gave me a grin to spur me on. That helped.

I was not far into my speech, talking about how hard it was entering a new scene, when it suddenly hit me that I didn't want them to feel like I did when I first came. I don't know how it all got linked up in my brain, but it all seemed similar: the shock of entering a new country, going interstate, moving from country to city, from school to work or uni—wasn't it all the same? The new is always an alien environment and none of us takes easily to change.

I could see them all watching me. Danny, with his hand in Vasa's: would he end up taking on his father's market garden? He didn't want to. Blake: would he get into flying school this time? And Sal, one of Danny's friends who had only recently declared she was a Torres Strait Islander: would she become a social worker and help the Indigenous street kids as she wanted?

Some had apprenticeships promised, others hoped their marks would be high enough to get into that course in uni they were after. Whatever they did, it would be strange, difficult. What if they didn't make it? I put my notes down. I didn't care if this didn't turn out to be a proper speech. I focused on the scariness of starting a new venture—a topic I knew heaps about.

'When I came at the beginning of the year, it was like journeying into a new world. Everything was strange, nothing turned out as I'd expected. It felt like I was out in the dark and I'd lost my life on the ground and I couldn't see to pick it up.' I hadn't meant to get so personal but it all kept tumbling out. 'And I don't want you to feel like that.

'If I can get through this year and stand here, saying this to you, you can get through all the changes that are coming.'

I told them what I had learnt about coping: the people who'd helped and the opportunities Australia had offered. I even spoke of the racial attack. 'I think if that had happened earlier in the year, I would have given up, but fortunately I'd been here long enough to know not everyone stalks around waiting for migrants or refugees to beat up. I've learnt that there's good and bad in every country. We need to make the most of the good parts and change the bad.'

I paused and suddenly Blake was standing, clapping in that slow way Ukrainians do in their dances. Then Danny stood, and Vasa, and Sara, then everybody. Ten months ago, they hardly knew me and no one except Danny would have supported me like that.

Blake came up to the microphone then. 'I reckon we've found another rep for next year's student council.'

When the clapping had died down, the band started playing again. Then Blake took my hand.

'Let's dance?' I could only nod as he led me down onto the wooden dance floor. 'You did great. I knew you would.'

'Thanks.'

'Your outfit's cool too. It's like you—sort of Australian but a little mysterious and Eastern all the same.'

What does a girl say? I preferred stable ground so I moved onto a safer topic.

'I'm going back, you know.'

He seemed so startled I was sorry I hadn't explained better.

'Just for a holiday. My parents think it'll help me get my perspective straight.'

'Isn't it dangerous?'

'I'll be picked up by friends and taken to the mountains where it's quieter. The media here makes it sound like the Taliban or ISIS is everywhere. Don't worry, I'll be back for Year 12.'

He looked as though he wanted to say something, yet thought better of it. Had he been looking forward to seeing me in the holidays?

'Is there something wrong?'

'No, everything's sweet.' He smiled at me then and I knew it was just for me. All we needed was a skateboard and we'd be winging through the sky, over the outback Australia that I'd never seen and where he probably spent his holidays.

The music became slower and he stepped in closer. Suddenly I was too aware of him, like the time he first found me in the library, but this time I had no regrets. I wasn't scared and I hadn't worn plaits.

As his arm came around me for the waltz he bent his head to my ear so I would hear. 'Don't forget to come back, Jaime.'

More from Rosanne Hawke

Beyond Borders : The War Within

Australian teenager, Jaime Richards, returns to her dear Pakistan in the second book of the Beyond Borders series. The old world charm is still there—the villages, the bazaars and the mysterious rugs—but Jaime no longer feels safe and confident in this new Pakistan.

Taken at gunpoint into Afghanistan, Jaime, Jasper and Liana are caught up in a shadowy secret world of intrigue and terrorism. Will they escape the Mujahadeen fighting their holy war? Or will the wars within themselves consume them?

For Jaime, this trip is to prove painful enough to change her life forever, yet rest the ghosts of her past.

Beyond Borders : Liana's Dance

After her international high school in Northern Pakistan is attacked by terrorists, sixteen-year-old Liana Bedford and the young music and dance teacher, Mr Kimberley must find a way to rescue student hostages who have been imprisoned in an ancient caravanserai. Liana discovers Mr Kimberley has a secret and to save him and her friends she must overcome her fears and dance for her life.

This is Liana's story as told by her friend Jaime Richards from *Dear Pakistan* and *The War Within*.

Zenna Dare

When Jenefer moves to the old family home in country Kapunda, she uncovers a secret from the past. What sort of life did Gweniver, her great-great-great-grandmother, lead? And what connection did she have to the glamorous young singer, Zenna Dare? Could a nineteenth-century mother of nine have led a double life, and if so, why?

In a story crossing five generations, from Cornwall and the old world to Australia and the new, Zenna Dare brings reconciliation in more ways than Jenefer could ever have imagined.

This accomplished novel parallels a 19th century and a contemporary love story, and canvases racism, reconciliation and the power of forgiveness. Jenefer resents being relocated to her family's ancestral home at Kapunda, but her imagination is caught by a model cottage that houses all the elements of a family mystery, and her heart by Caleb, a poised, perceptive Aboriginal classmate. This richly textured tale of family relationships and changing morality across two centuries is both enthralling and thought-provoking.

Katharine England, The Advertiser.

About the Author

Rosanne Hawke is a South Australian author of over 25 books, among them, *Zenna Dare*, *Mustara*, shortlisted in the 2007 NSW Premier's Literary Awards, *The Messenger Bird*, winner of the 2013 Cornish Holyer an Gof Award for YA literature, and *Taj and the Great Camel Trek*, winner of the 2012 Adelaide Festival awards. Rosanne was an aid worker in Pakistan and the United Arab Emirates for ten years and now teaches creative writing at Tabor Adelaide. In 2015 she was the recipient of the Nance Donkin Award for an Australian woman author who writes for children and YA.